LAZY DAISY

written by David Olson • illustrated by Jenny Campbell

DISCARD

 Ideals Children's Books • Nashville, Tennessee

an imprint of Hambleton-Hill Publishing, Inc.

To my mom and dad, who told me I could do anything.
—D.O.

For Mom, Scott, Amy and the roadrunner, and my whole Ohio family.
—J.C.

Published by Ideals Children's Books
An imprint of Hambleton-Hill Publishing, Inc.
1501 County Hospital Road
Nashville, TN 37218

Library of Congress Cataloging-in-Publication Data:
Olson, David J.
 Lazy Daisy / written by David J. Olson ; illustrated by Jenny Campbell.-- 1st ed.
    p. cm.
 Summary: Lazy Daisy is proud to have the messiest room in the world until it swallows her grandmother and her closet belches out enough junk to bury the whole town.
 ISBN 1-57102-162-0 (hardcover)
 [1. Laziness--Fiction. 2. Orderliness--Fiction. 3. Cleanliness--Fiction. 4. Tall tales. 5. Stories in rhyme.] I. Campbell, Jenny, ill. II. Title.

PZ8.3.O498 Laz 2000
[E]--dc21

                                                                00-029558

First Edition

The illustrations in this book were rendered in watercolor.
The text type is set in Souvenir.

Cover and book design by
John Laughlin

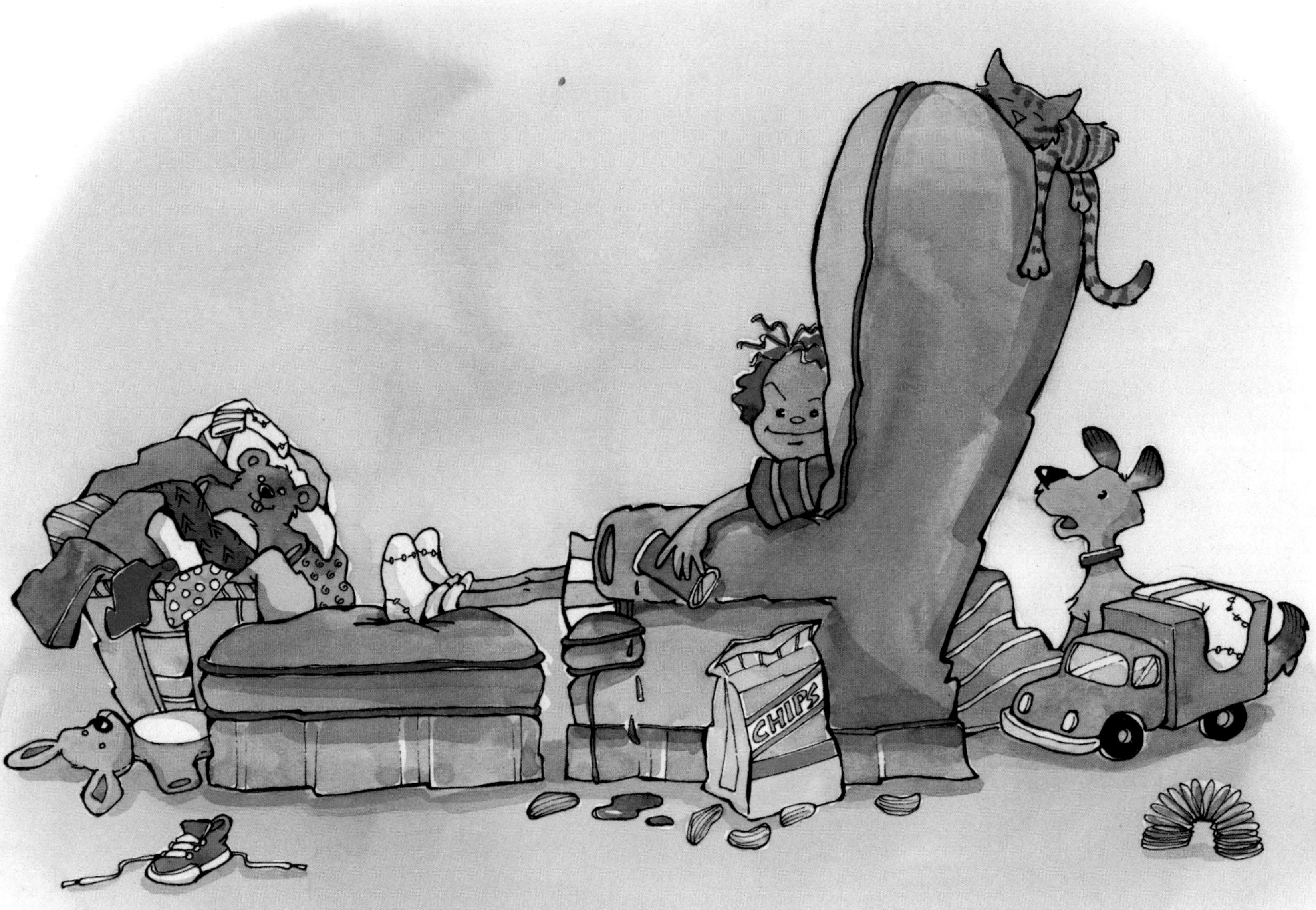
CHIPS

Pay close attention young girls and young boys,
for here's a sad story of laundry and toys.
There once was a child who called herself Daisy,
and Daisy was super fantastically lazy.

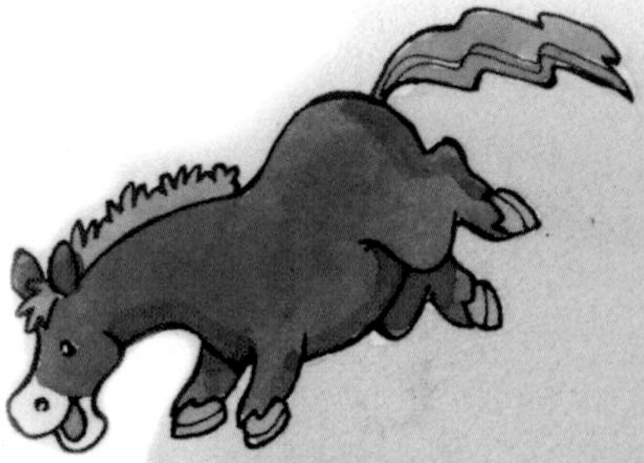

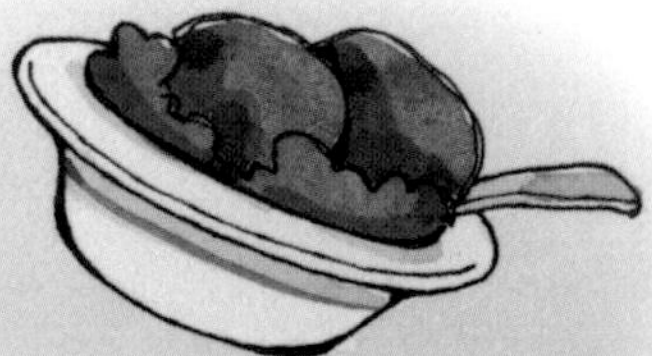

"I'm Lazy Daisy!" the child would scream.
"I'm perfect as ponies and chocolate ice cream!
I'm better than angels and blackberry pie
and I'll never work 'til the day that I die!"

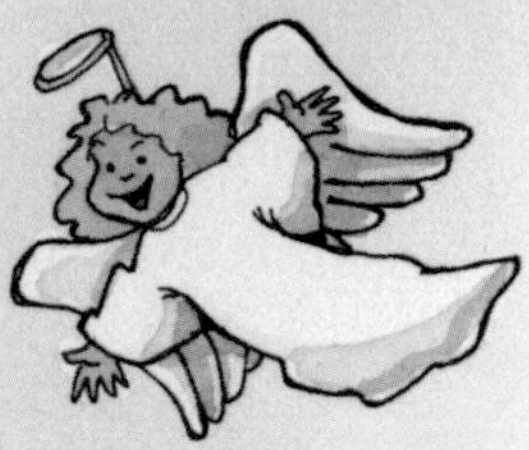

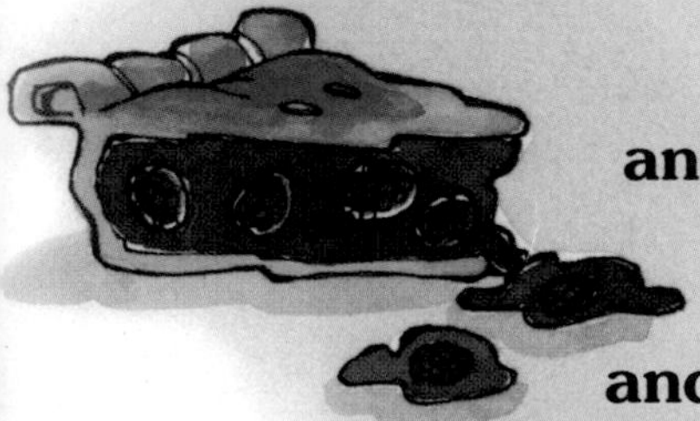

To bite on her nails she hired her brother,
and oatmeal was spooned to her lips by her mother.
She trained her iguana to buckle her sandals,
and on birthdays her hair dryer blew out the candles.

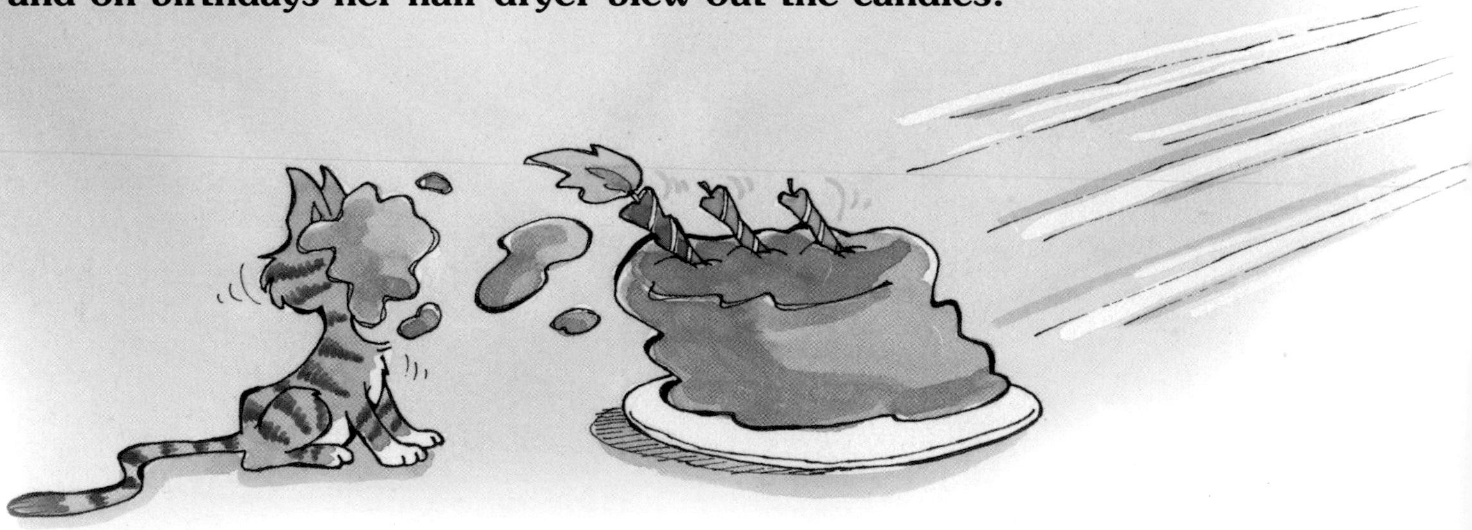

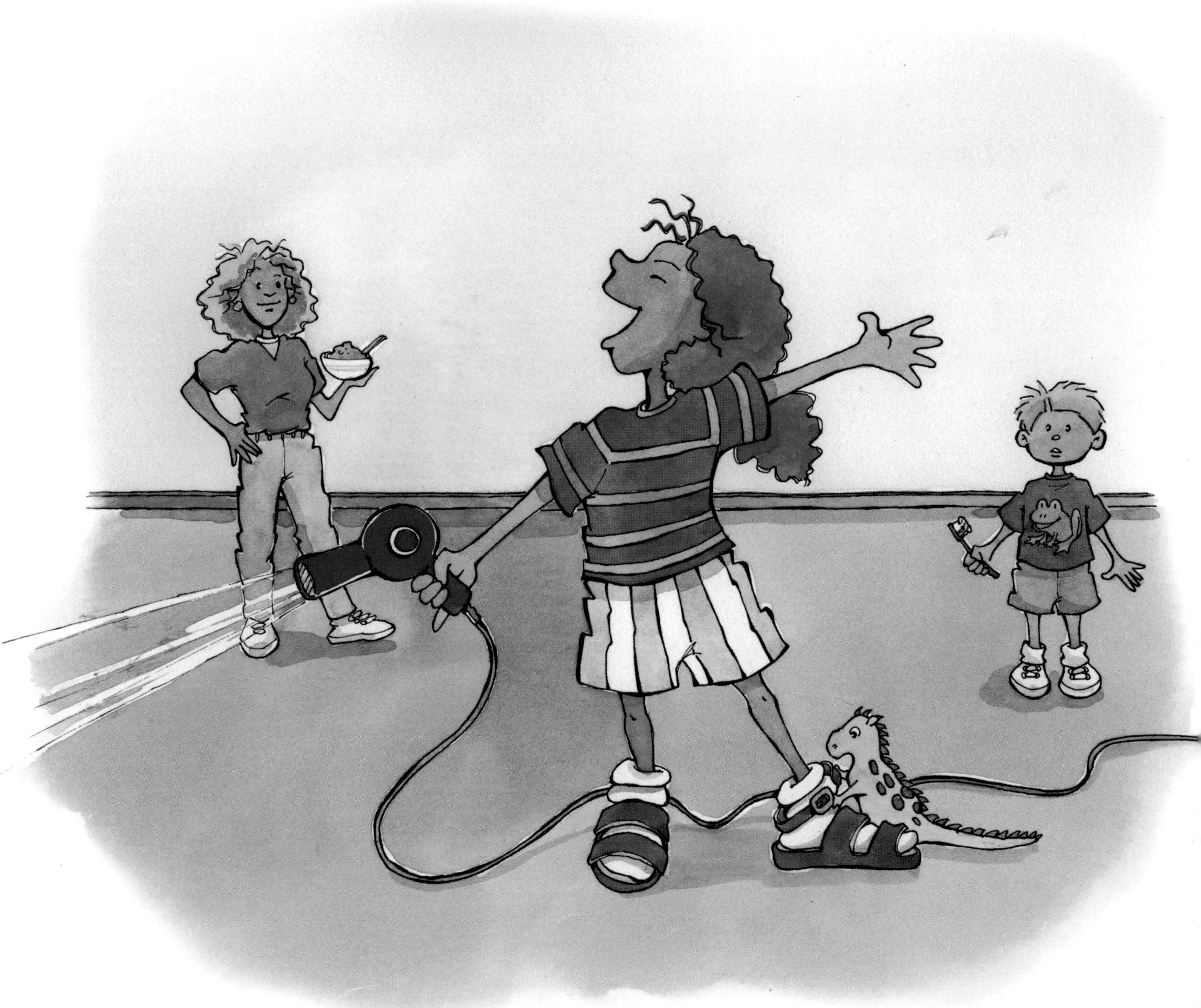

But the thing that would finally seal Daisy's doom
was the fact that she simply would not clean her room.

"I'd rather eat turtle tails," Daisy would say,
"or punch a gorilla from southern Bombay!
On stilts I'd walk backwards to El Salvador
before I'd pick up all the toys on my floor."

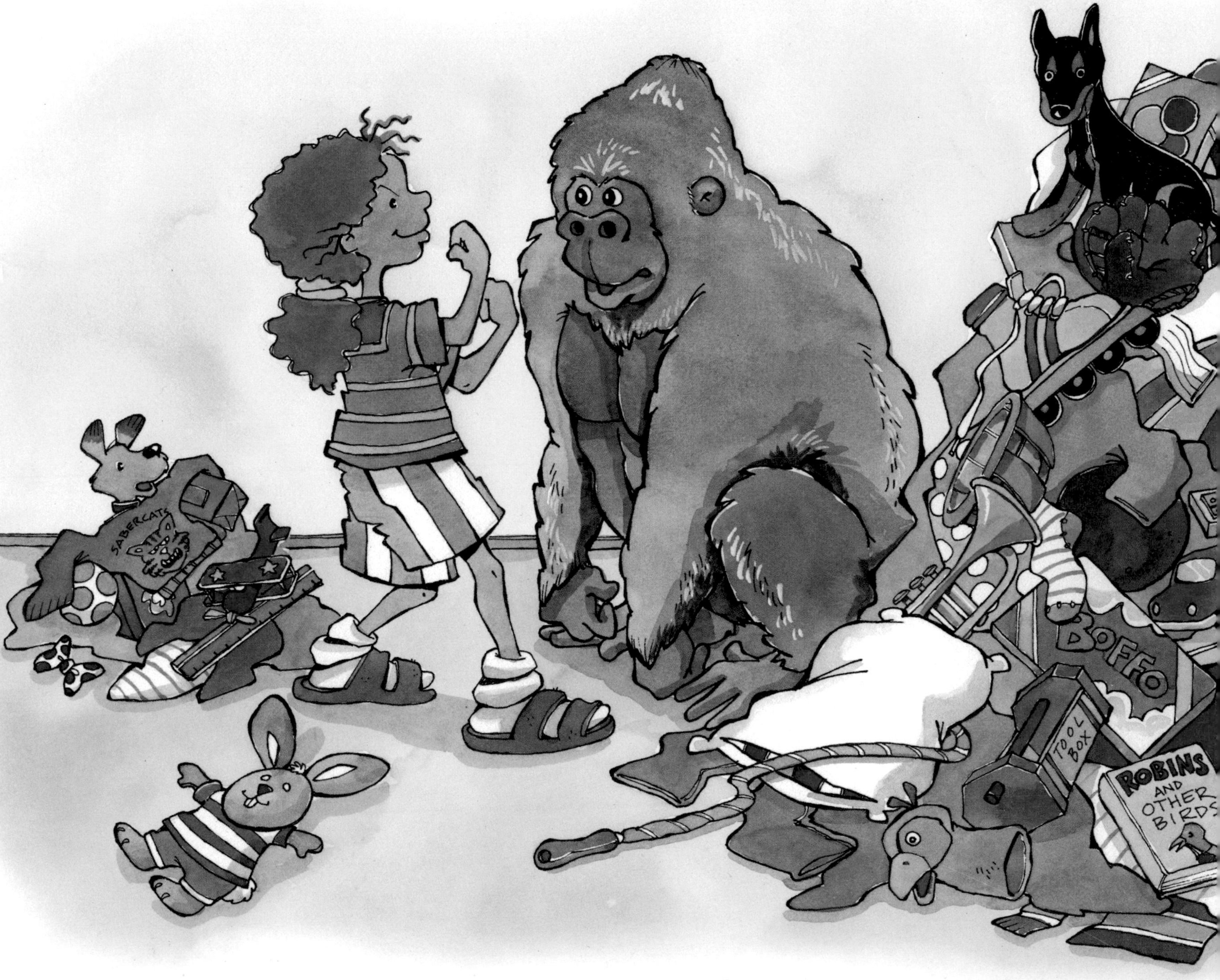
SABERCATS
BOFFO
TOOL BOX
ROBINS AND OTHER BIRDS

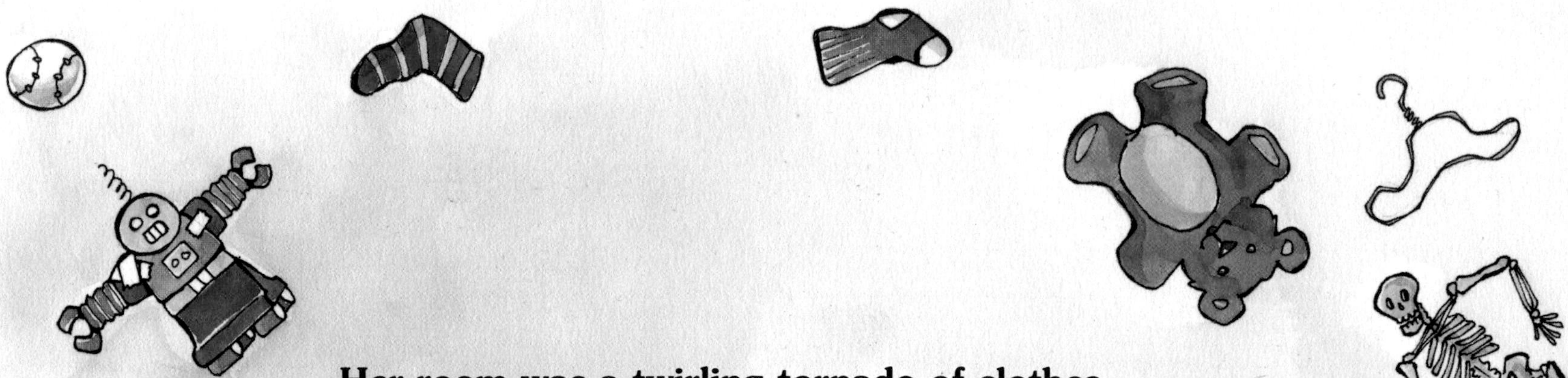

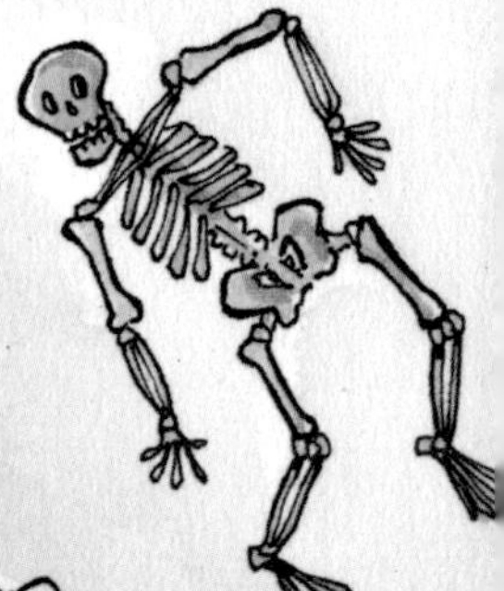

Her room was a twirling tornado of clothes
that made grown-ups shiver right down to their toes.
There were piles of blue jeans and lost underwear
and seventeen dollies without any hair.

Twisted up hangers all bent out of shape,
robots with arms held together with tape,
a teddy with beans falling out of his head,
and thousands of socks were heaped by the bed.

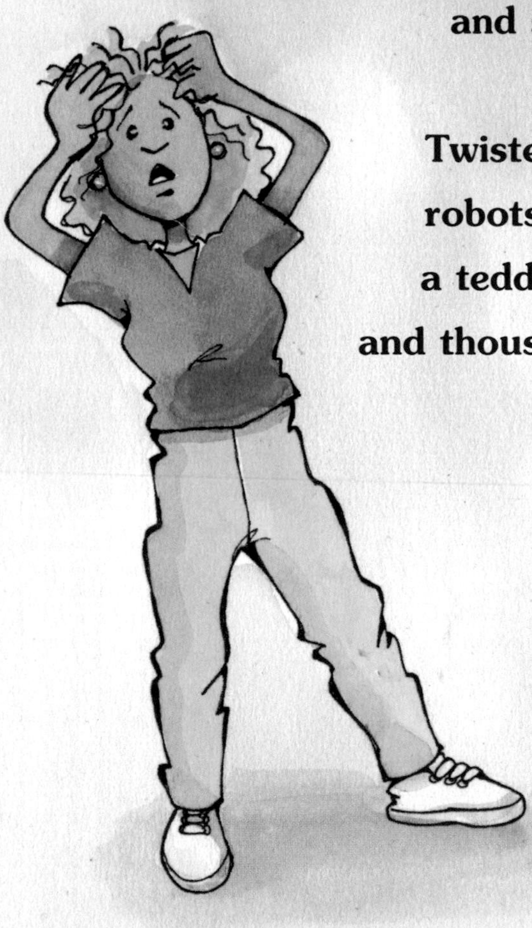

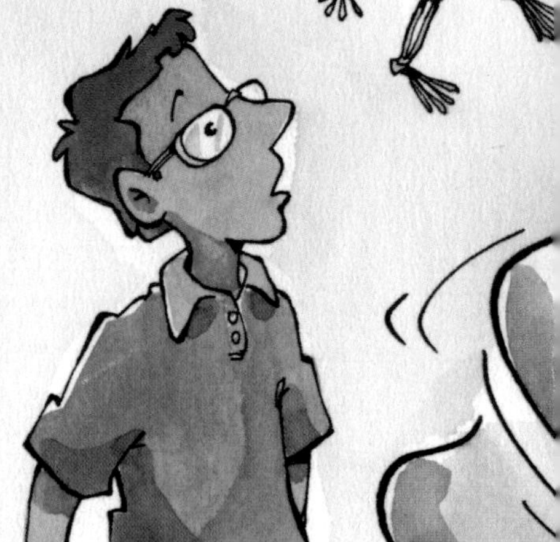

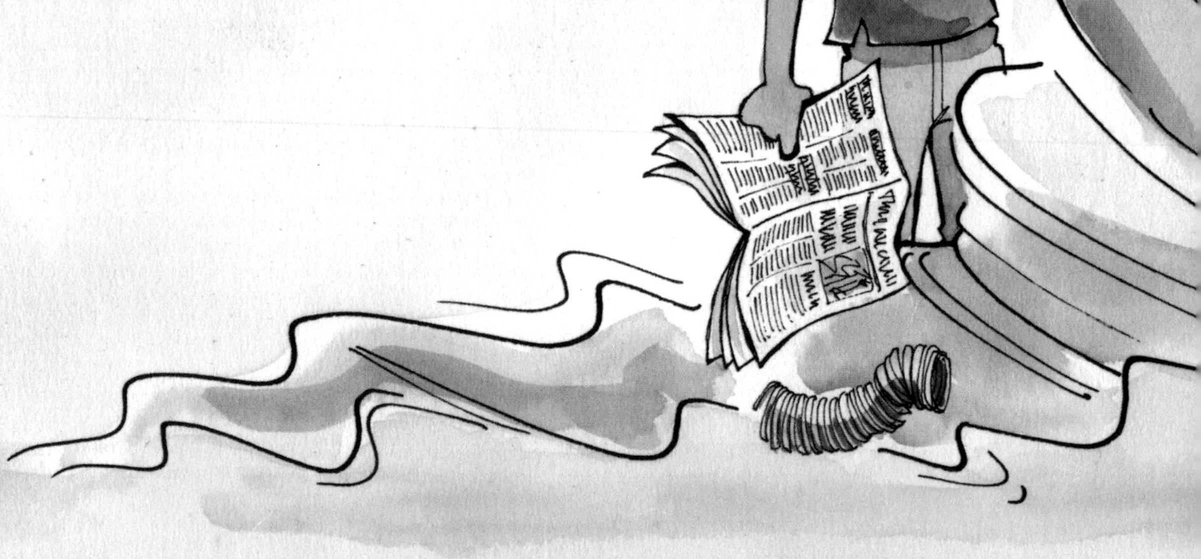

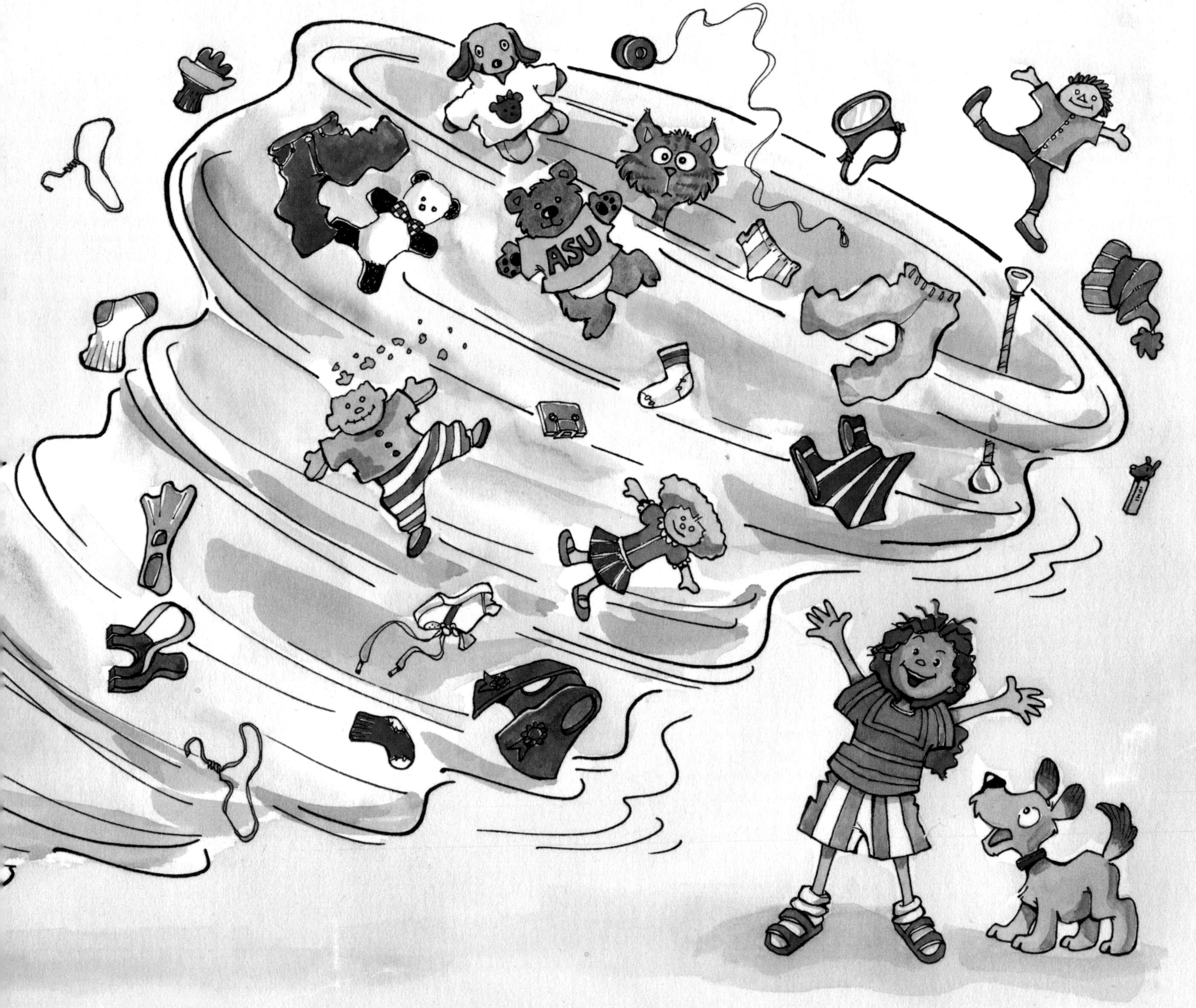
ASU

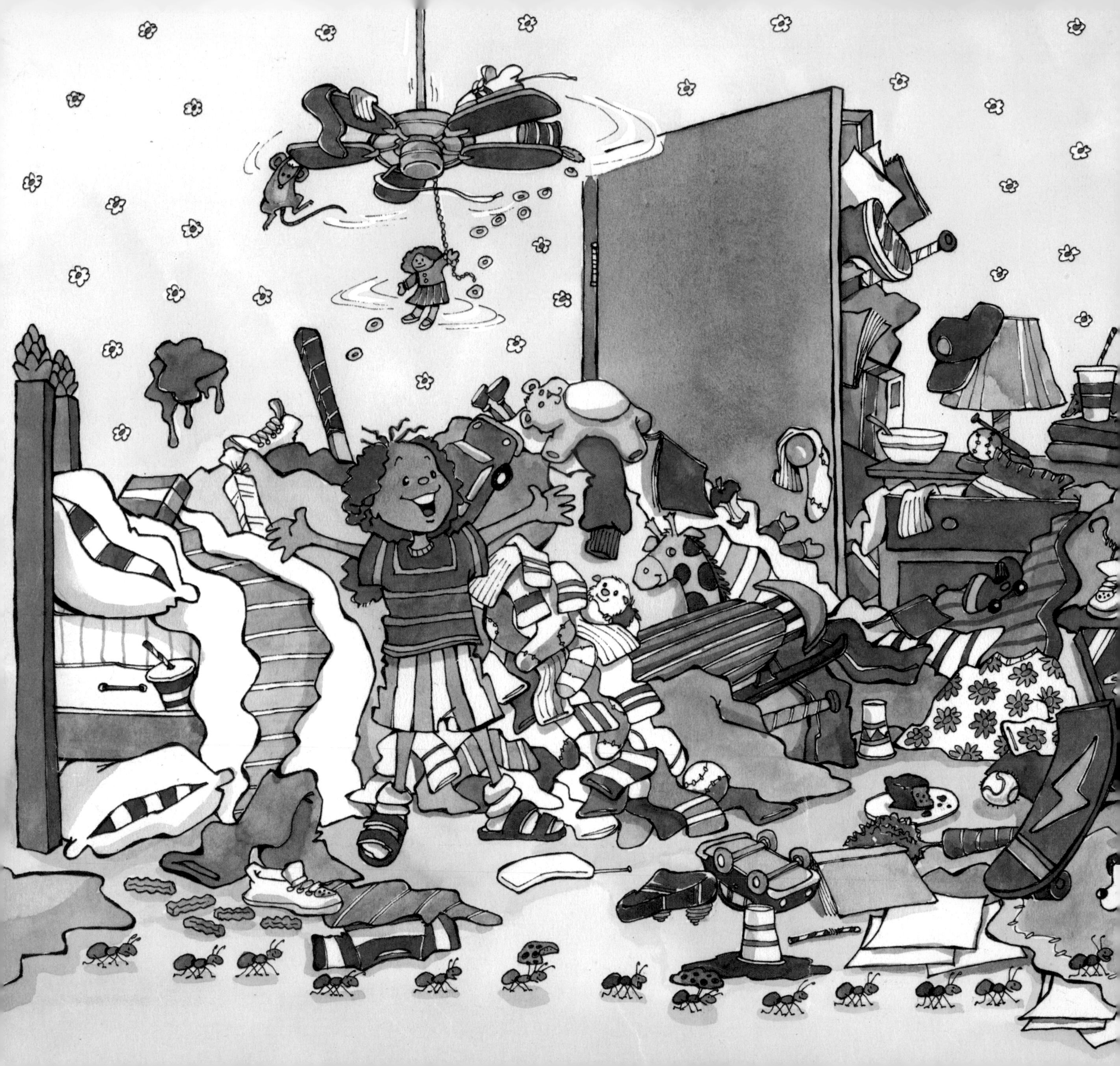

Hamsters and guinea pigs lived on the run
in the room that sparked memories of old World War One.
There were crumbles of cookies and spilled carrot stew,
and hundreds of armies of ants marching through.

"My room is the messiest room in the world!"
Daisy declared as she tip-toed and swirled.
"Mom wants it tidy, but I could care less!
NOTHING COMPARES TO MY MARVELOUS MESS!"

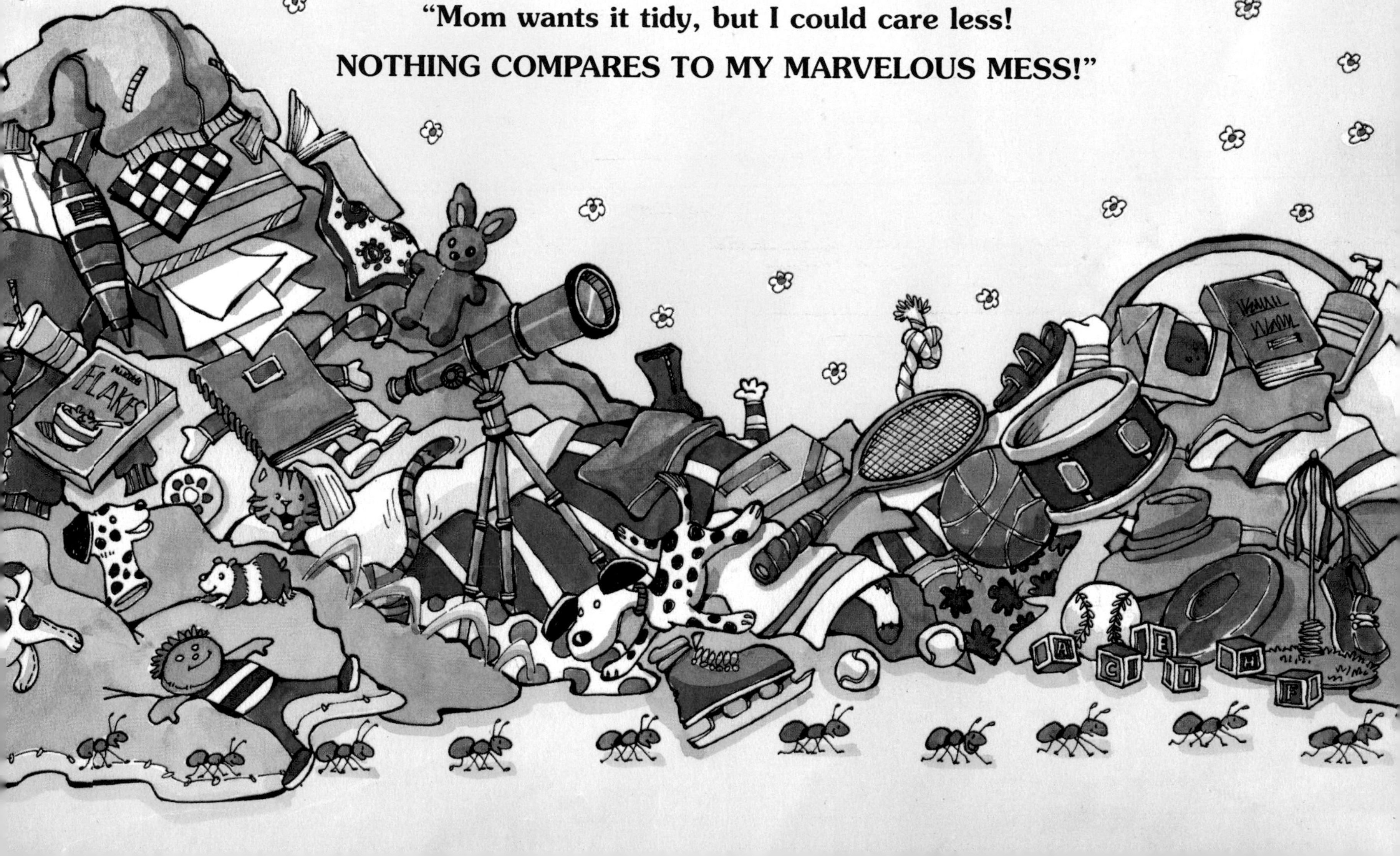
FLAKES

Now messes are ugly
and sometimes they stink,
but messes are harmless...
so most people think.

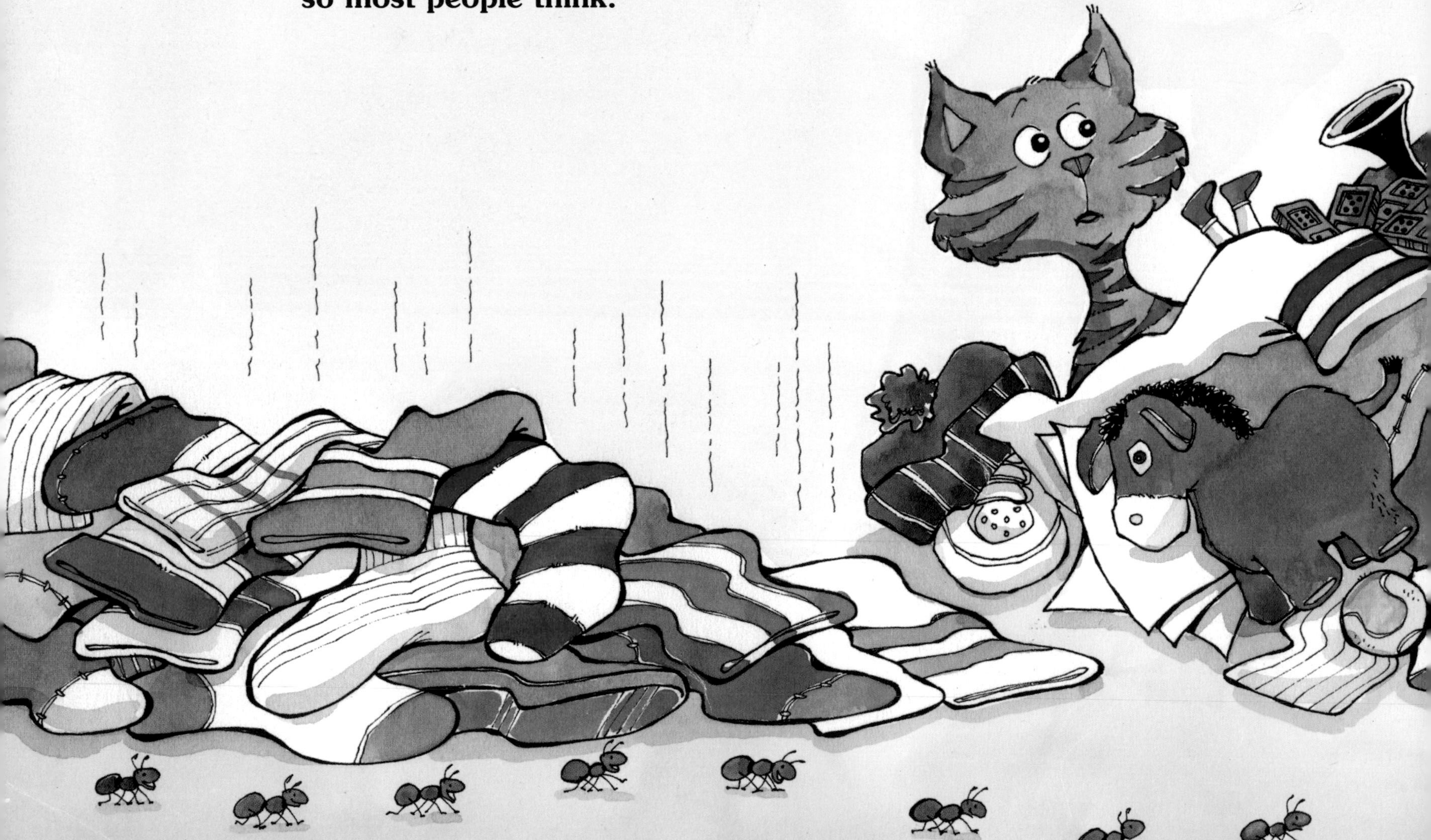

But one crazy night in the middle of May,
when Daisy's poor Gramma drove over to stay,
something went haywire, something went bad.
Something ridiculous, something quite sad.

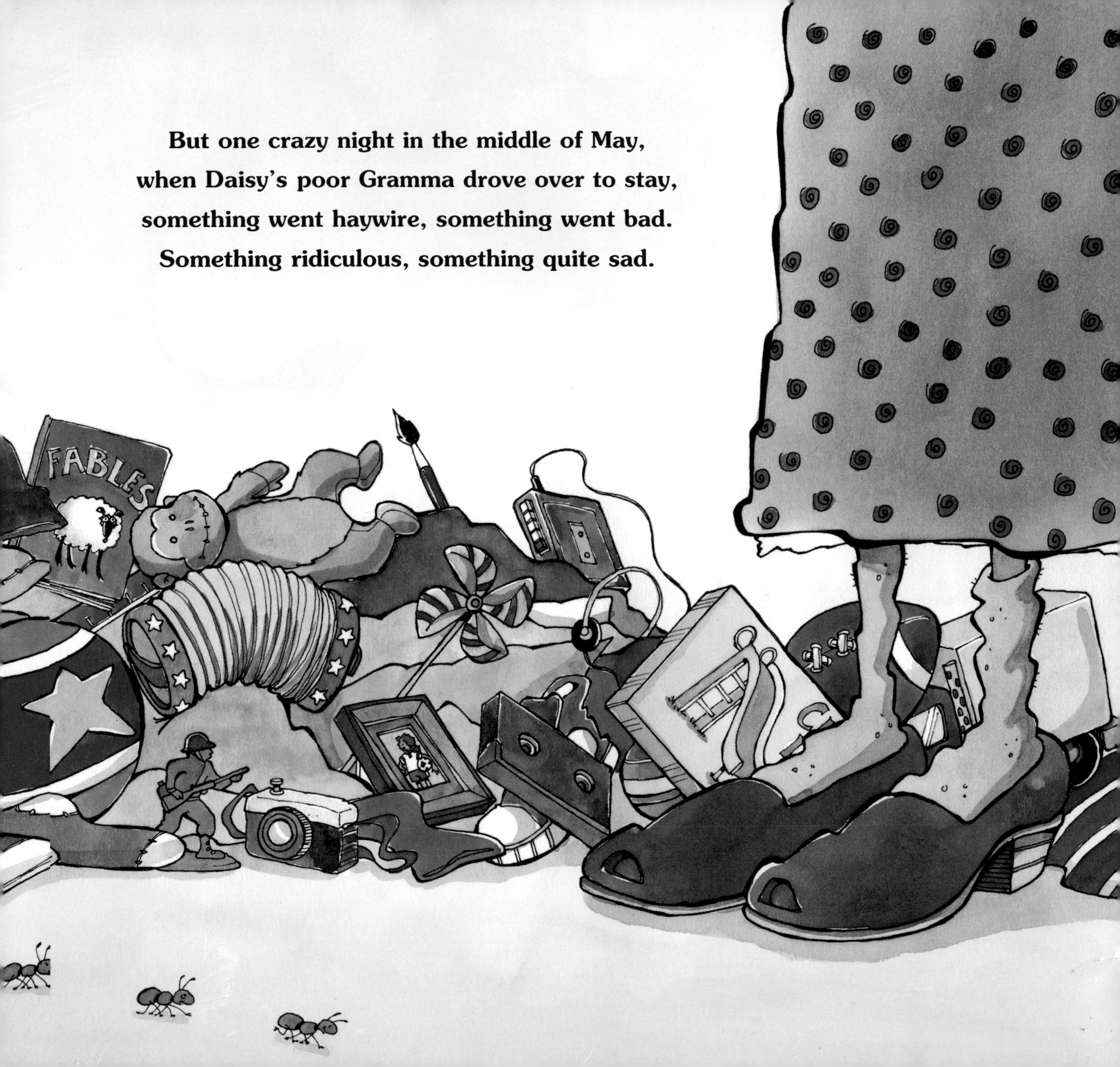
FABLES

At supper that night near a quarter to nine
just before Gramma slurped from her wine,
her dentures rocked loose and slipped to the floor
and bounced through the kitchen and out the back door.

"Follow those dentures!" her dear Gramma said,
"In the name of bananas and earthworms and bread!"
They hopped through the garden and sprung to the roof,
then down the brick chimney in a black cloudy POOF!

The teeth that had fallen from old Gramma's head
came to a rest underneath Daisy's bed.
"I'll catch 'em!" Gramma then shouted out loud
as she dove into the mess that made Daisy proud.

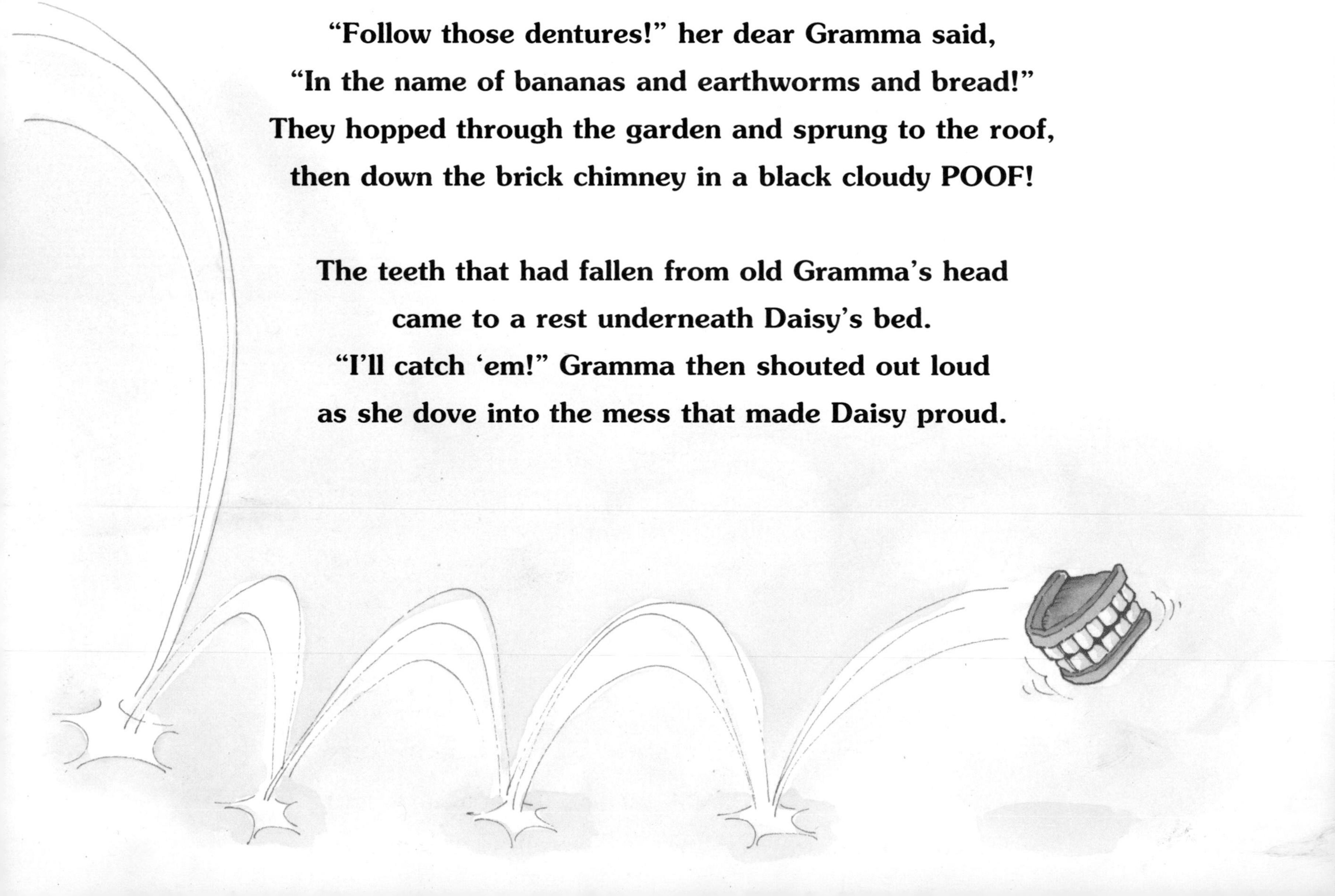

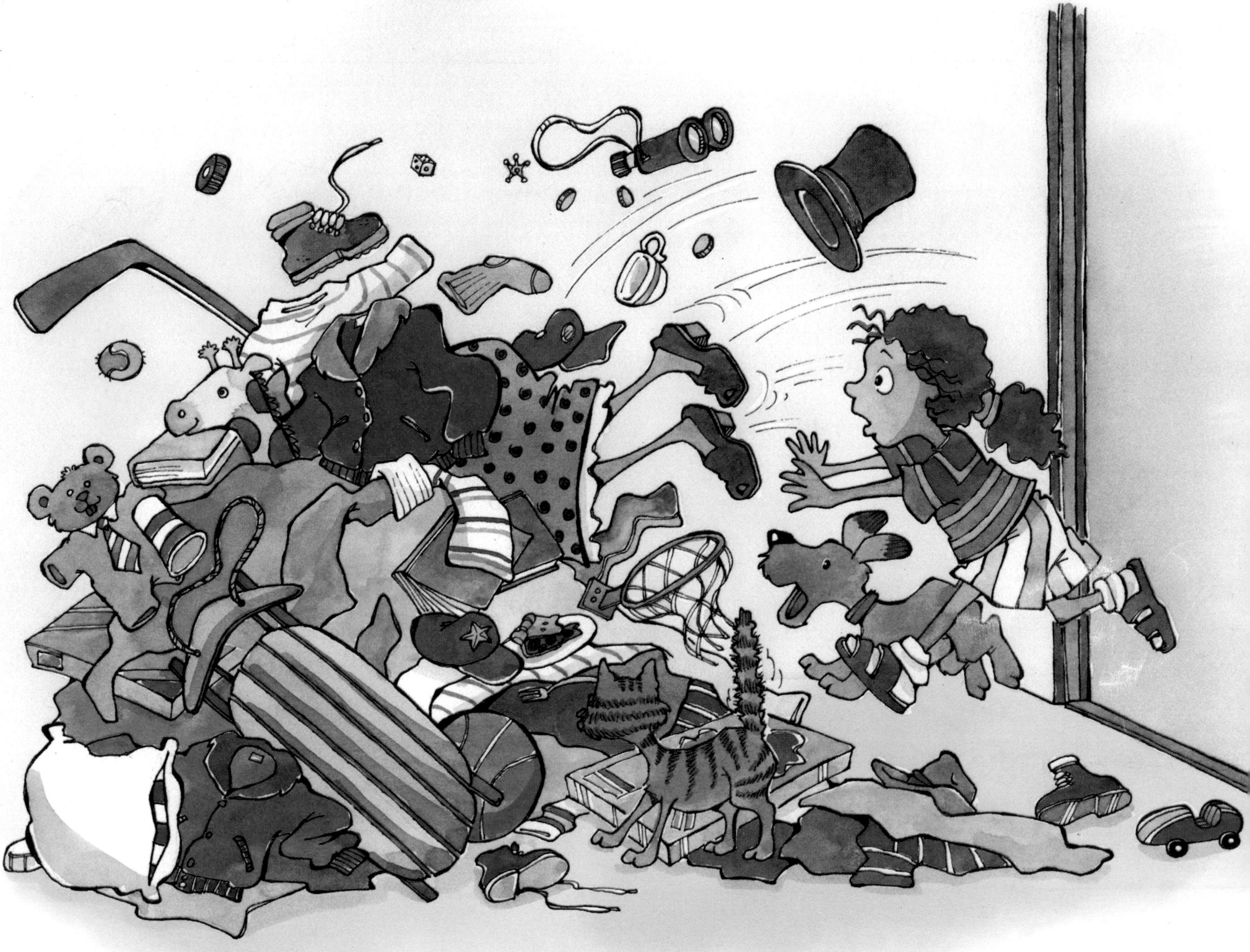

And just as you may have predicted or feared,
the toothless old grandmother... just disappeared.
That jungle of Daisy's was out of control.
It seized her dear Gramma and swallowed her whole.

"This is what happens to kids who are lazy!"
Mother declared to a weepy-eyed Daisy.
"I hope that for your sake your fingers are crossed
'cause right now it looks like your grandmother's lost!"

Daisy breathed deeply, said, "Fetch me a broom!
It's time I got busy and cleaned up my room."

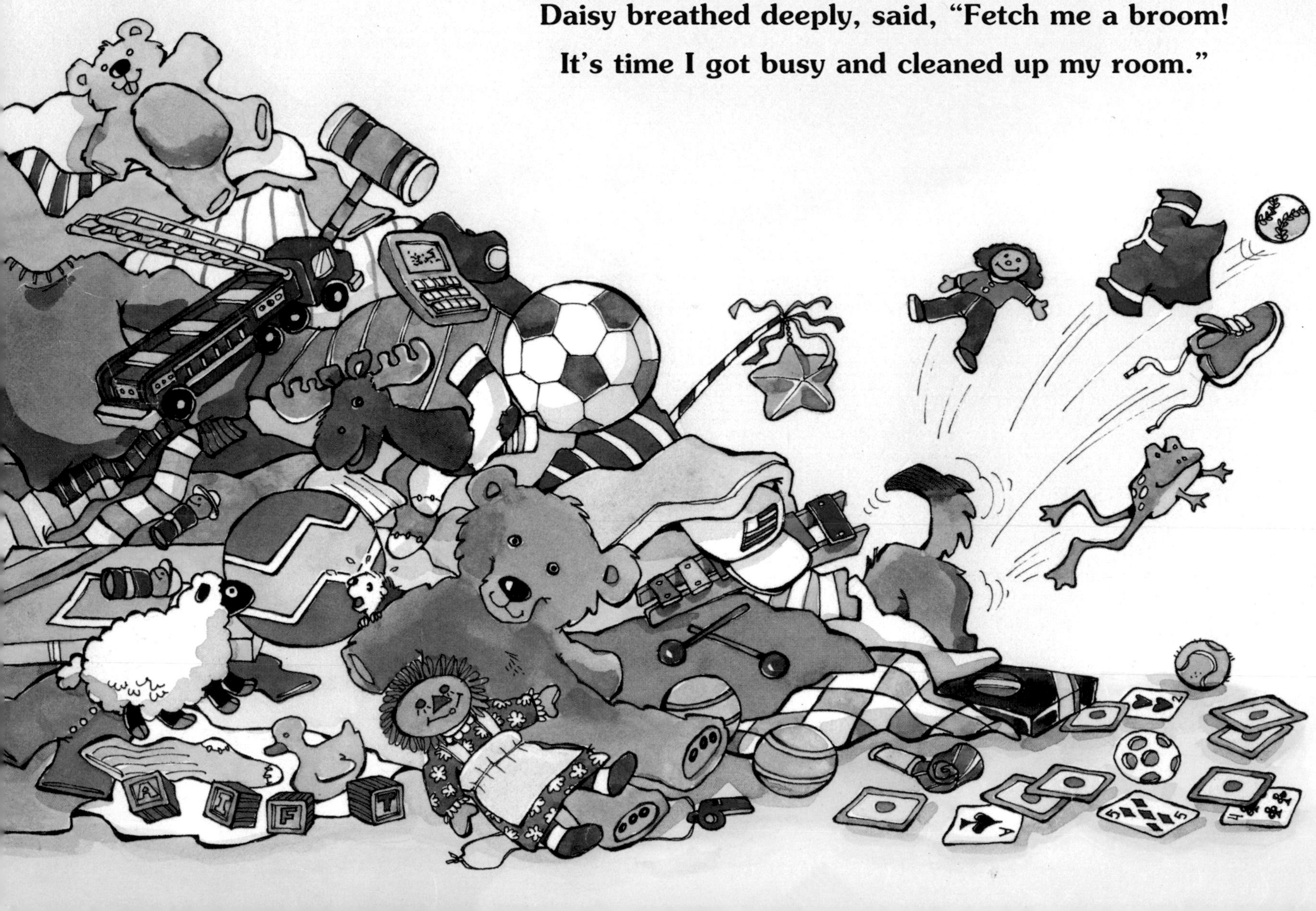

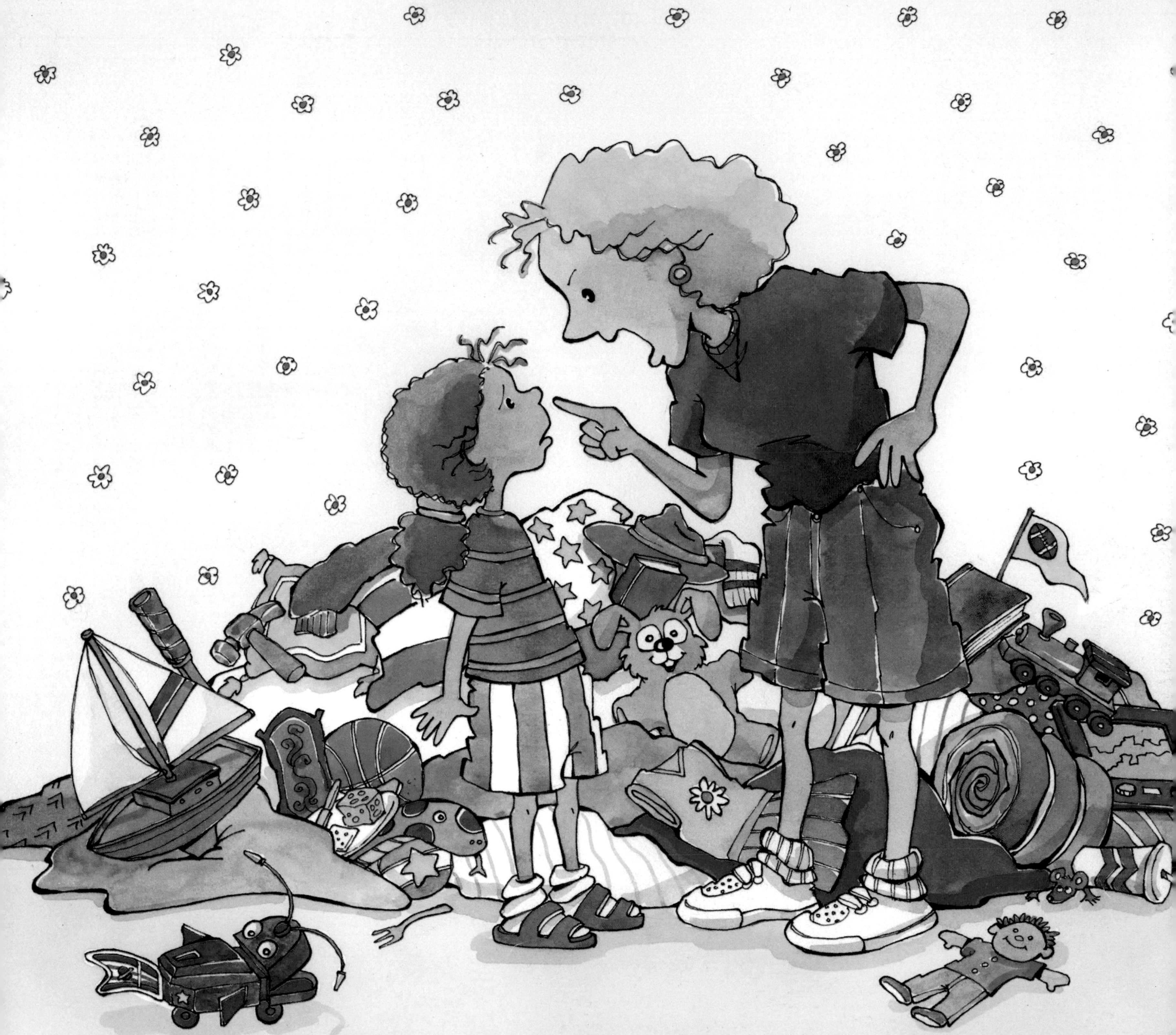

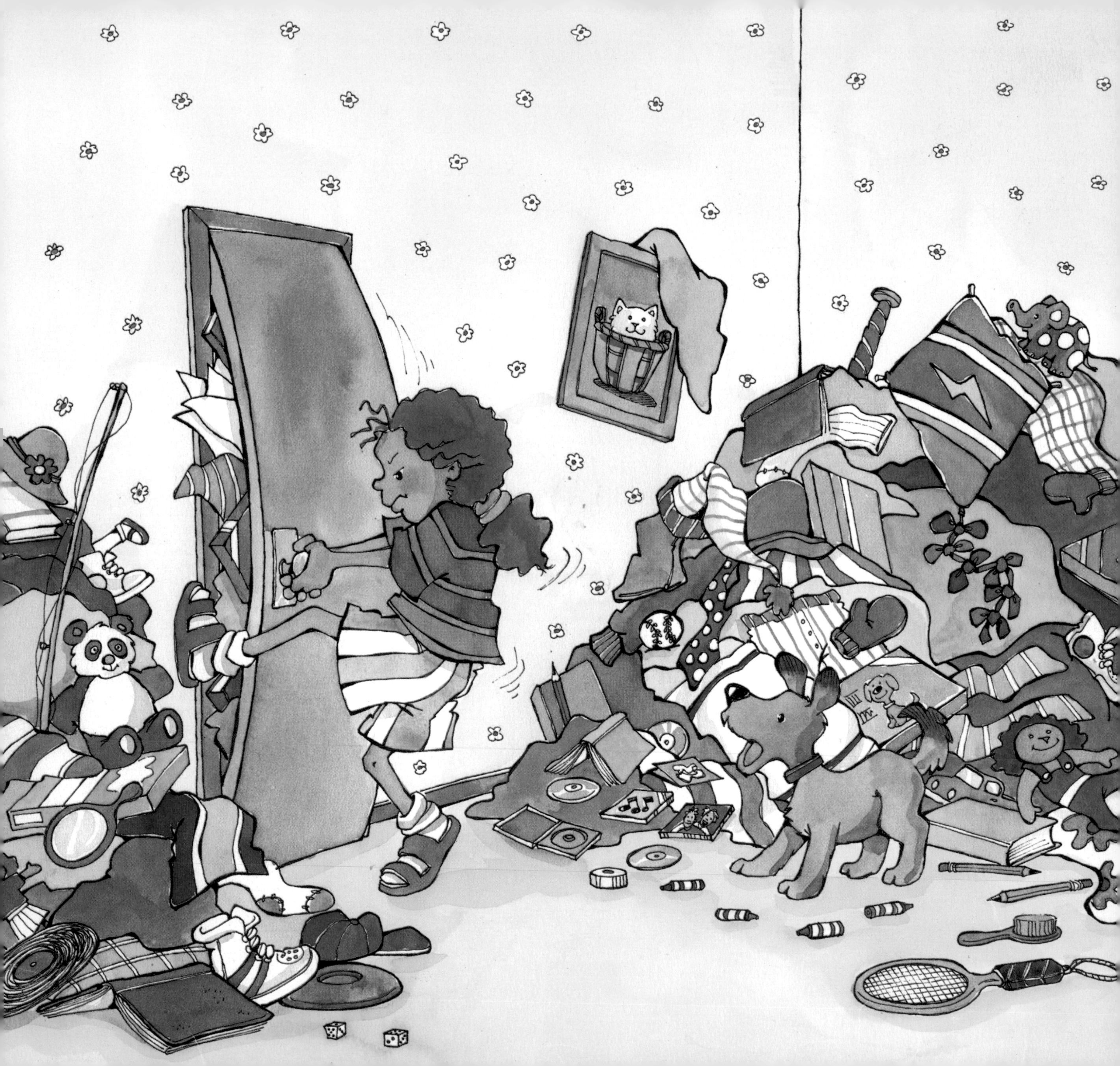

She dashed to the closet to start off the job,
arrived at the door, and twisted the knob.
The door didn't quiver, not rattle nor budge
for the hinges were knotted with string and hot fudge.

But... from deep in the walls came a grumbling sound
that shivered the windows and shook up the ground.
Daisy whispered a blessing and squeezed her eyes tight
and yanked on the doorknob with all of her might.

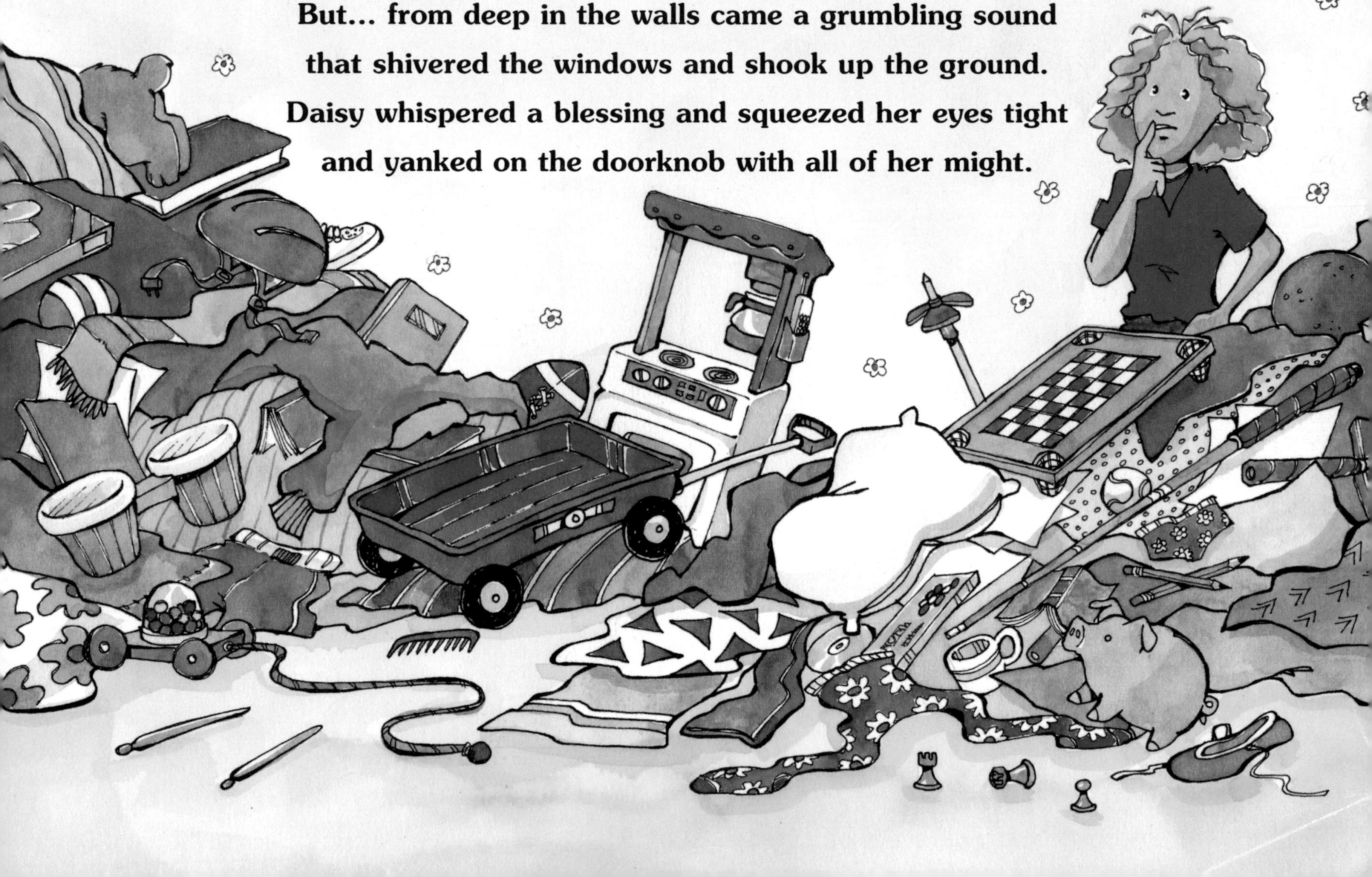

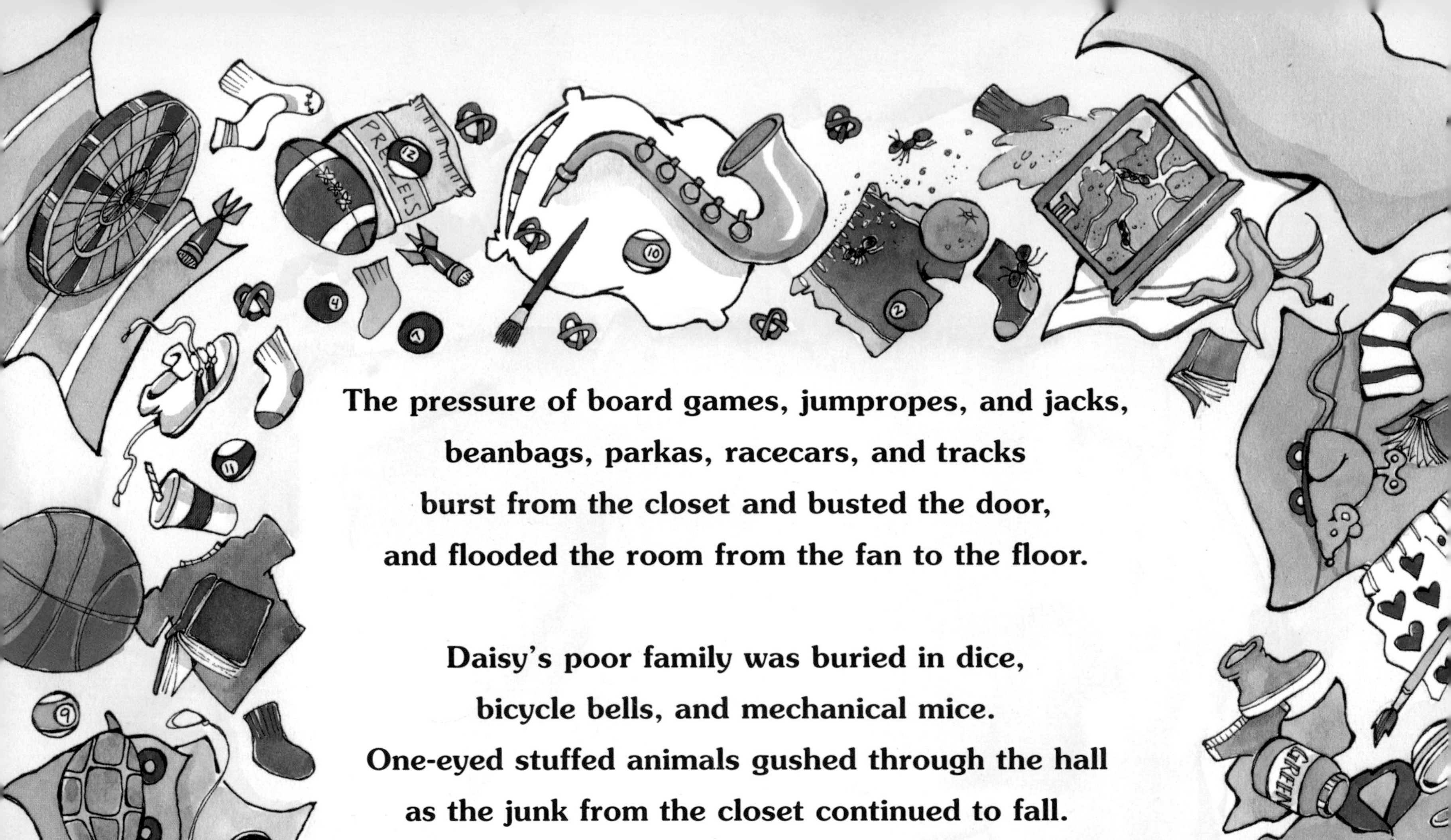
PRETZELS

The pressure of board games, jumpropes, and jacks,
beanbags, parkas, racecars, and tracks
burst from the closet and busted the door,
and flooded the room from the fan to the floor.

Daisy's poor family was buried in dice,
bicycle bells, and mechanical mice.
One-eyed stuffed animals gushed through the hall
as the junk from the closet continued to fall.

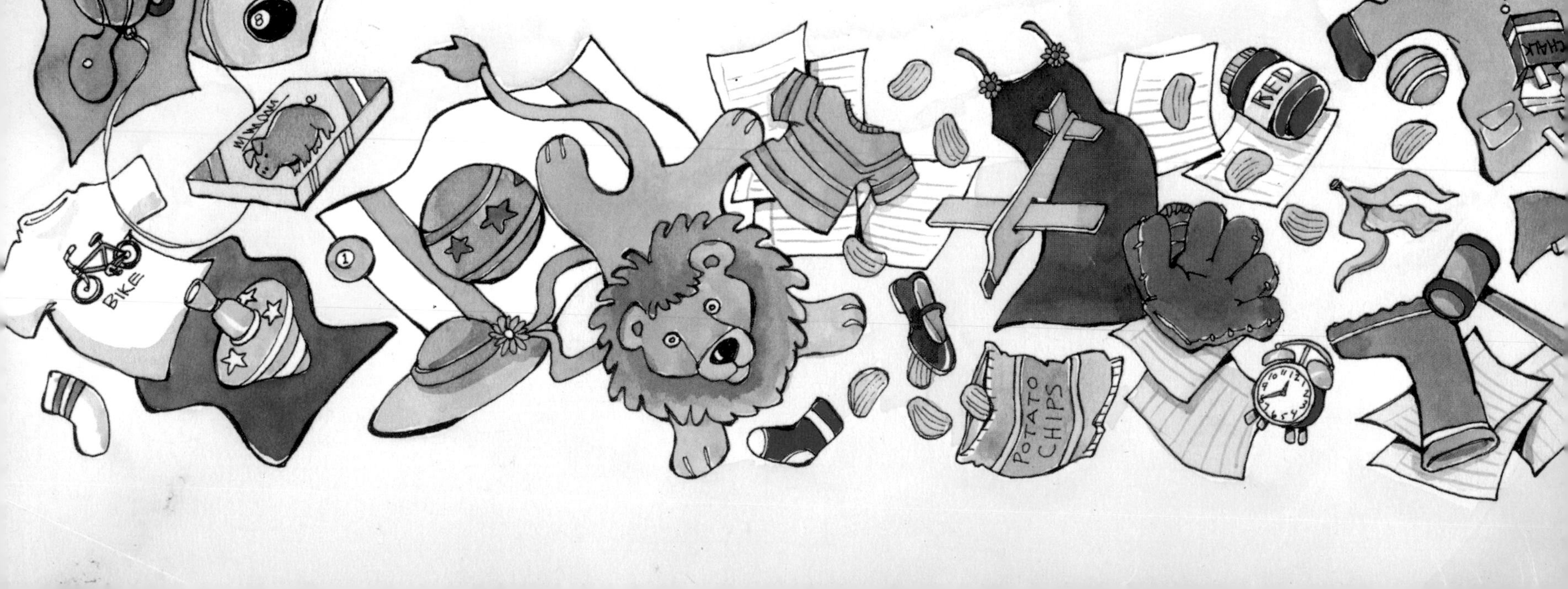
GREEN
CHALK
RED
BIKE
POTATO CHIPS

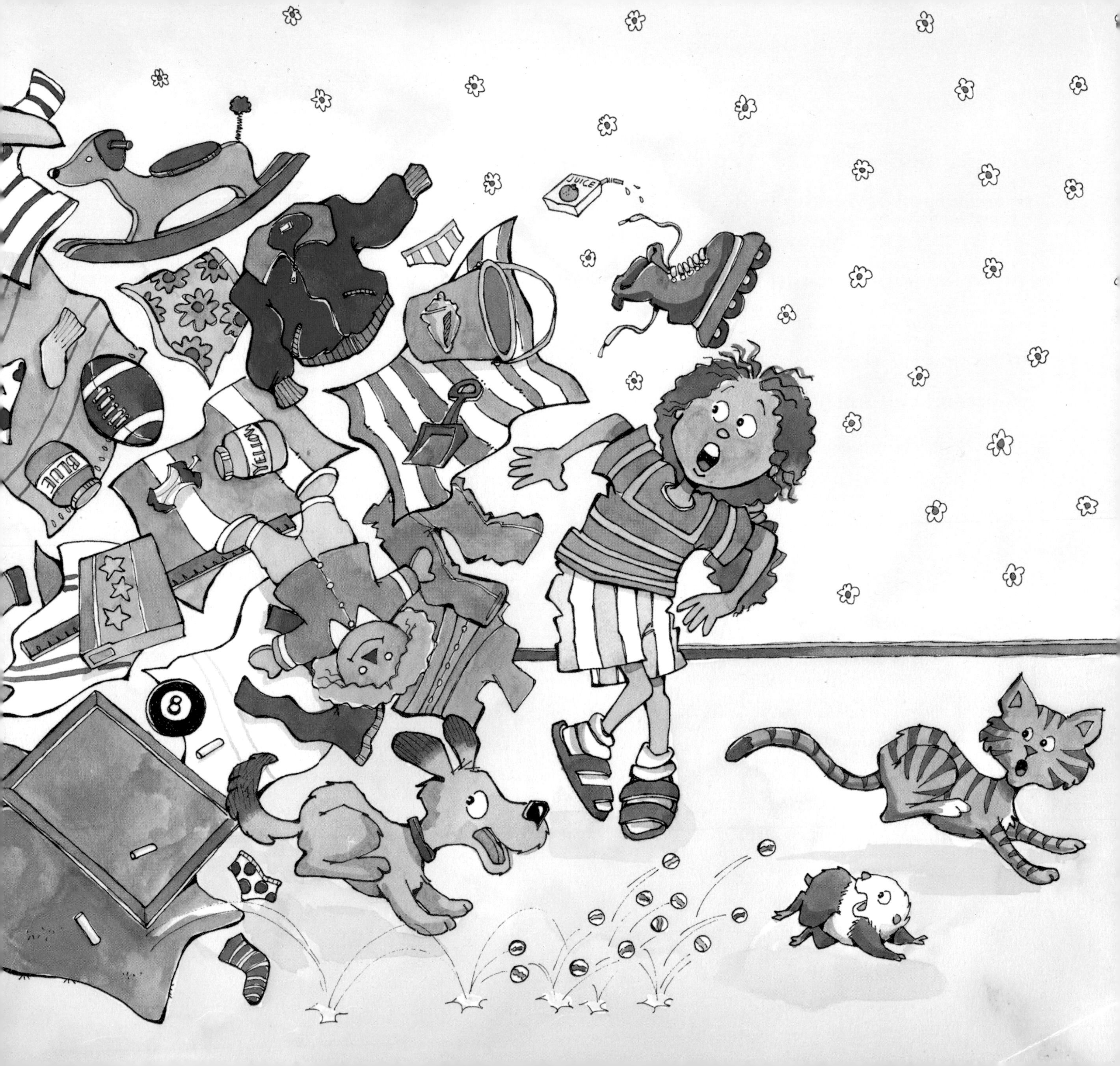
JUICE
YELLOW
BLUE

Peach pits and orange peels and half-eaten pears
and oval-shaped basketballs flopped down the stairs.
Daisy's glass windows were blasted to bits
by piggy banks, softballs, and wood-burning kits.

Squirt guns and checkerboards plunged to the yard
and buried the birdbath and pet Saint Bernard.
Puzzles and roller skates scattered the street,
but the closet's eruption was far from complete.

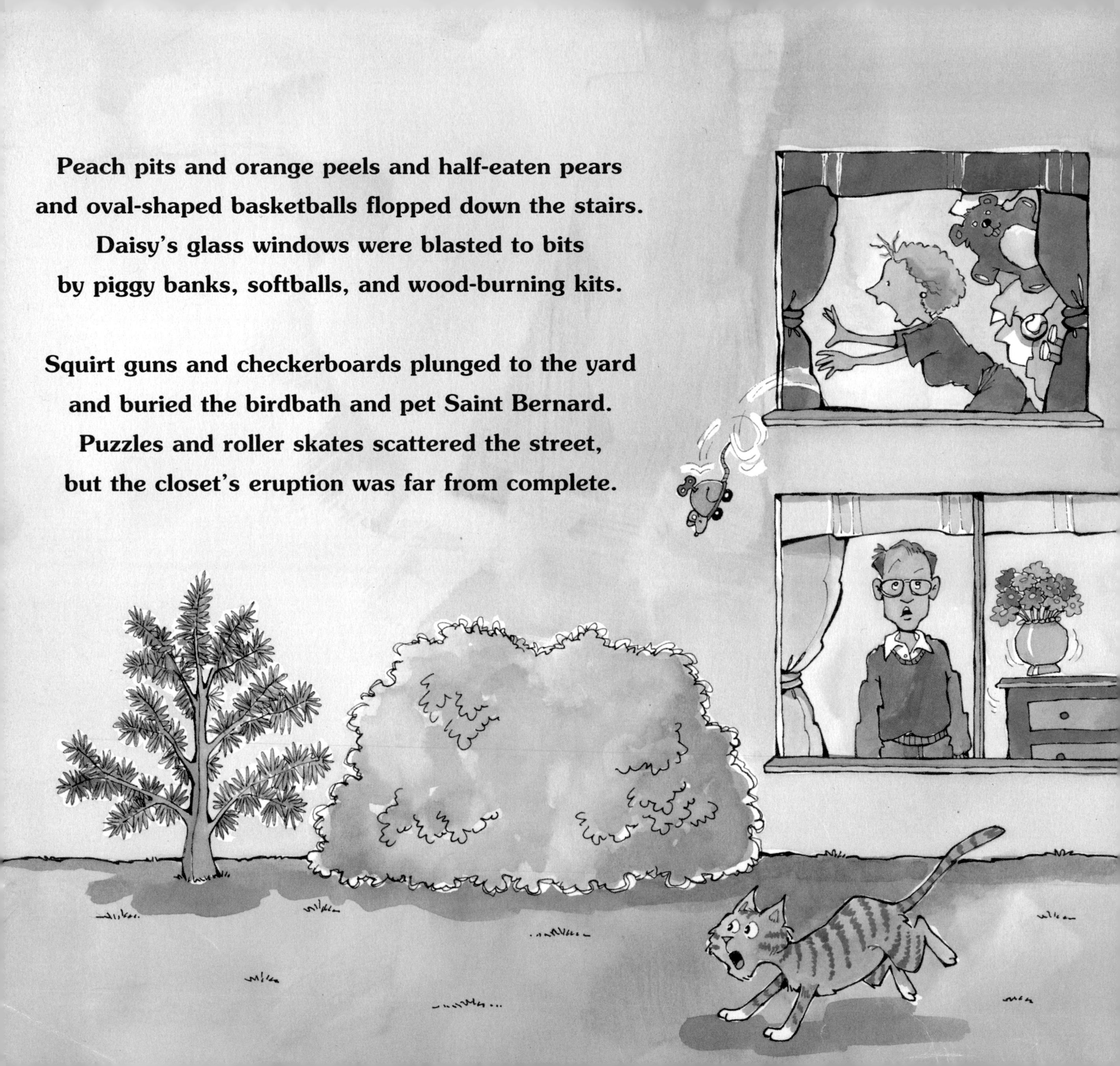

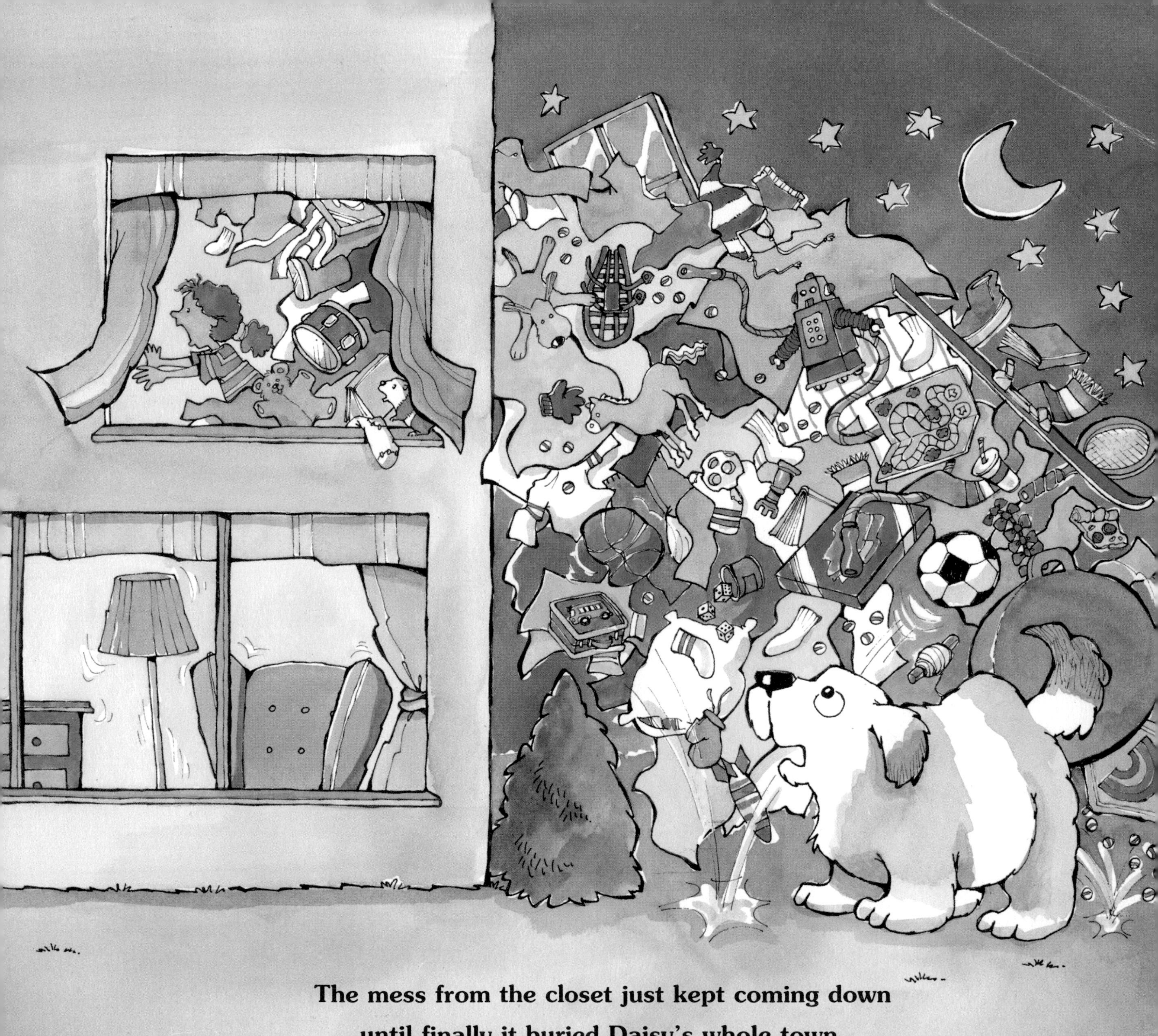

The mess from the closet just kept coming down
until finally it buried Daisy's whole town.

Mountains of underwear covered the school
and gold rubber duckies swamped every pool.
The subways were loaded with whiffle ball bats,
and shoes filled the sewers and buried the rats.

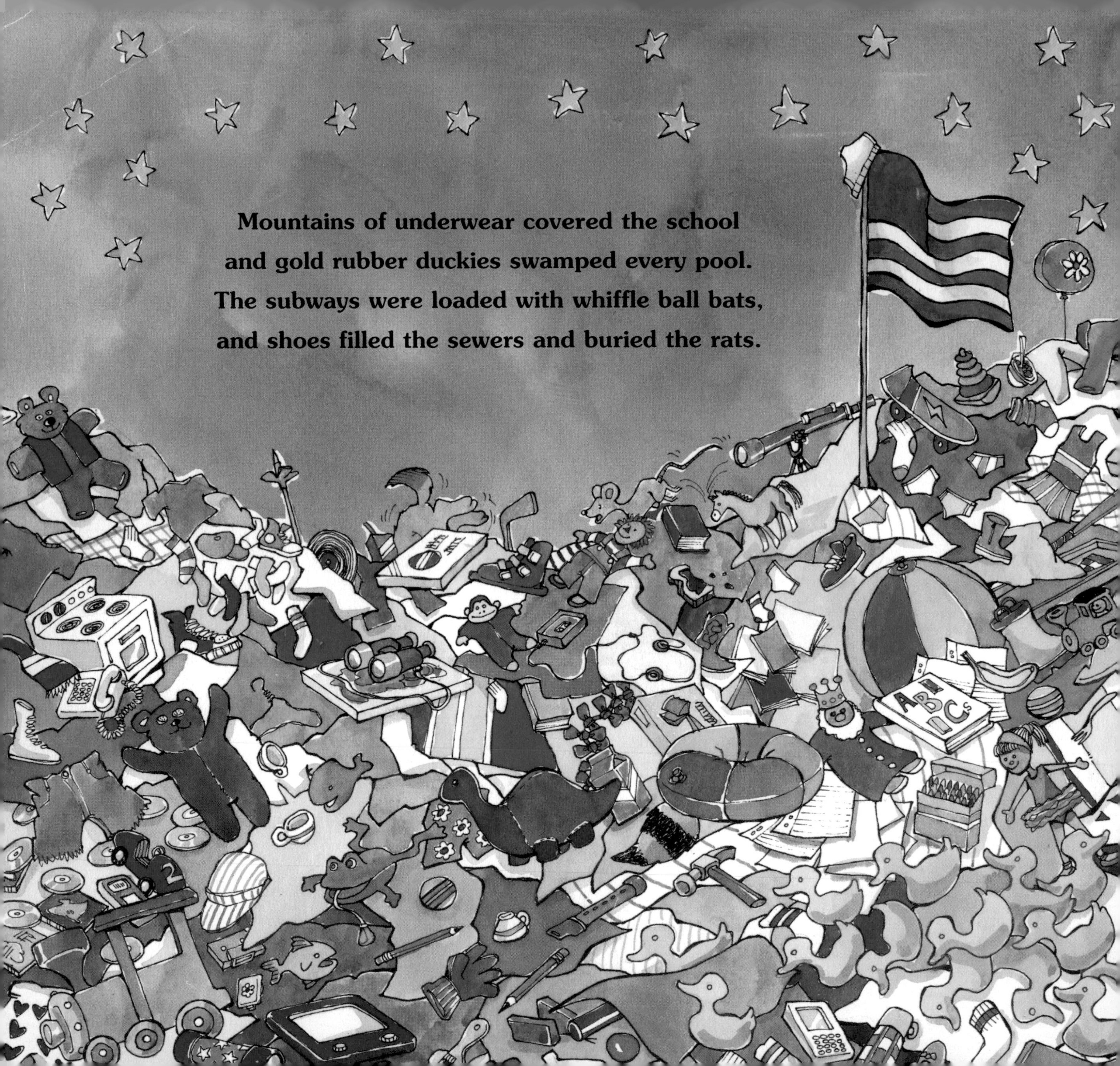

Comic books piled up layer on layer,
burying the new City Hall and the Mayor.
On Main Street where rush hour traffic once flowed,
nine thousand marbles spun loose down the road.

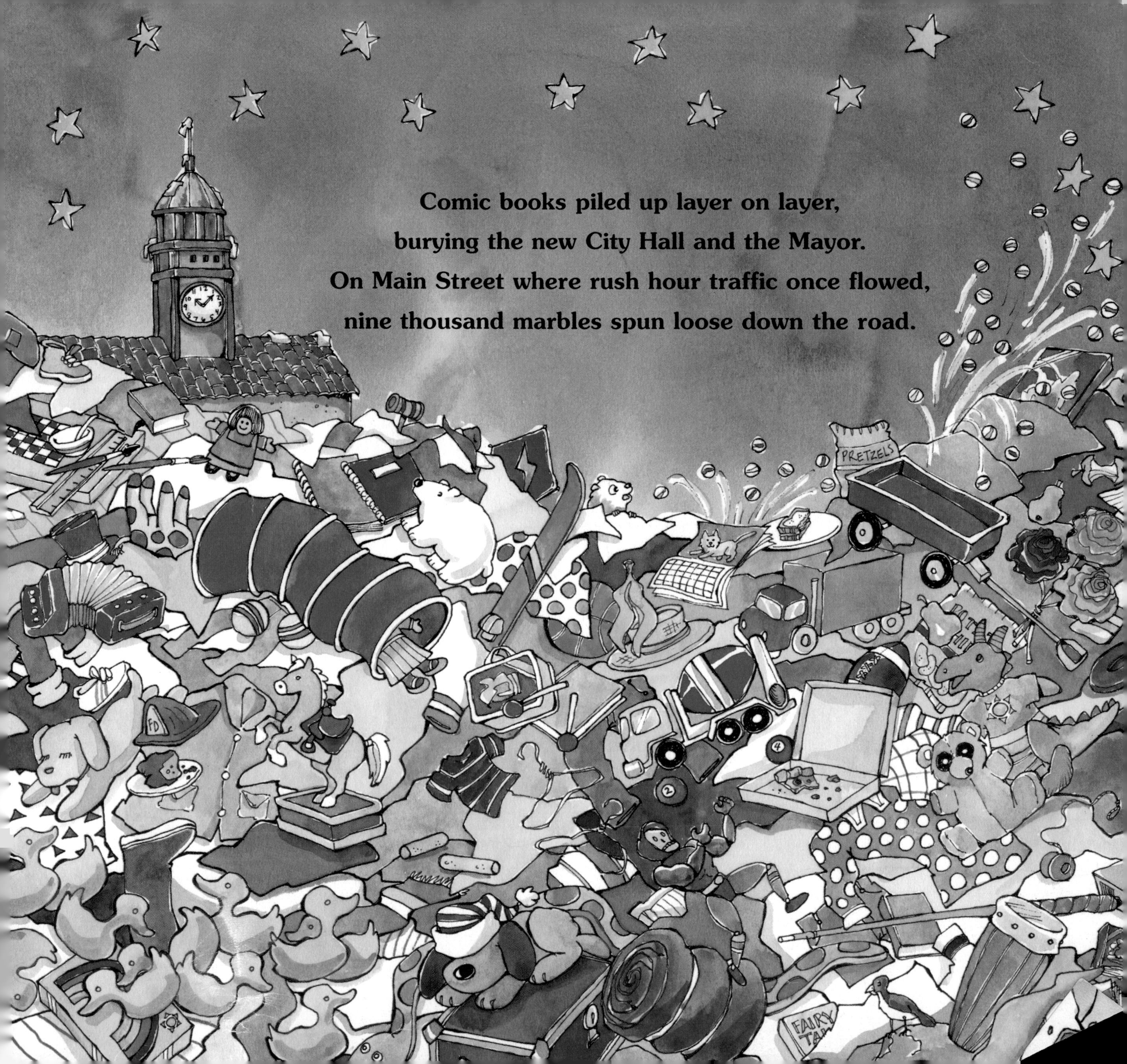
PRETZELS
FD

A hundred and eighty-two minutes went by
'til finally the mess was a half-mile high.
The last toy to fall from the closet that day
was a fat armadillo stuffed with dry hay.

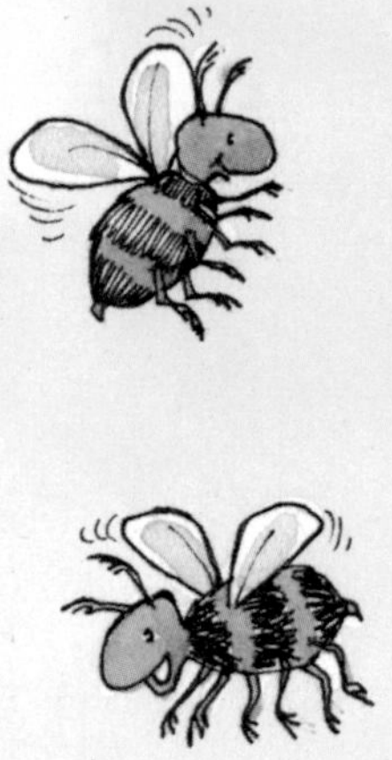

The city was silent except for the breeze,
the buzzing of bees, and the sneezing of fleas.

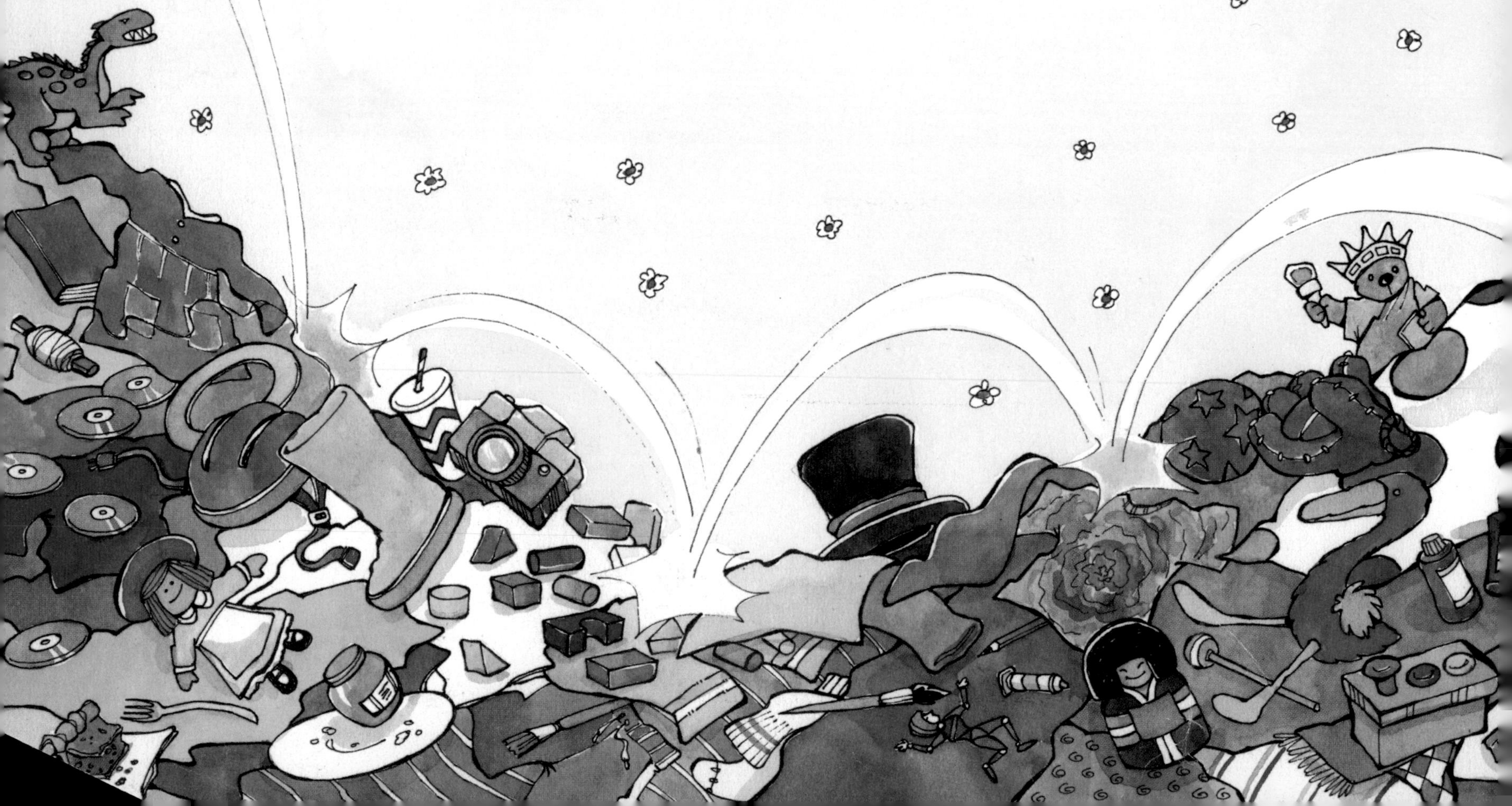

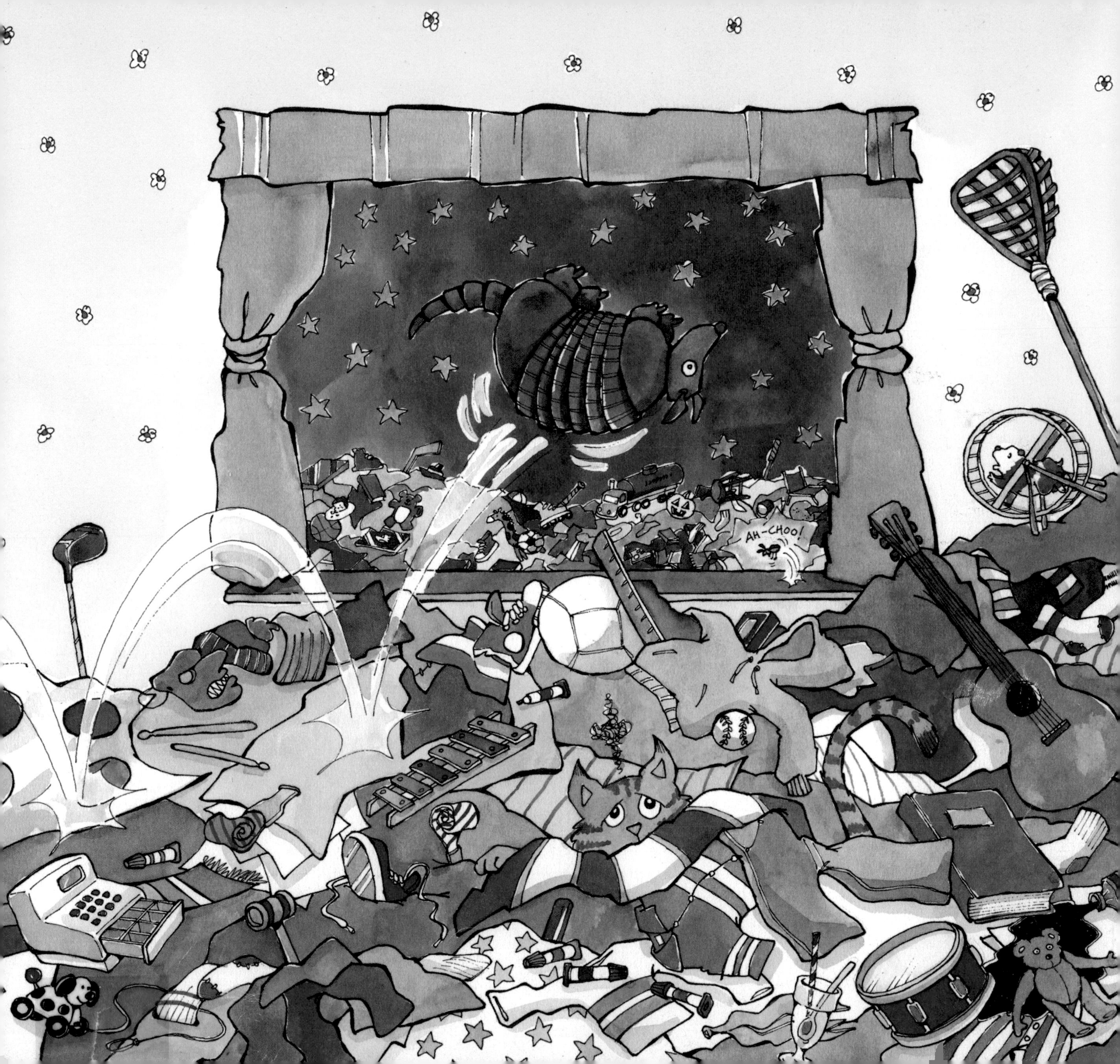
AH-CHOO!

But... all of a sudden from deep in the mess,
something popped up next to Daisy's address.
The sight that appeared was the raggedy face
of the laziest girl in the whole human race.

Daisy was shocked when she saw what she did.
Her heart felt like vultures, molasses, and squid.

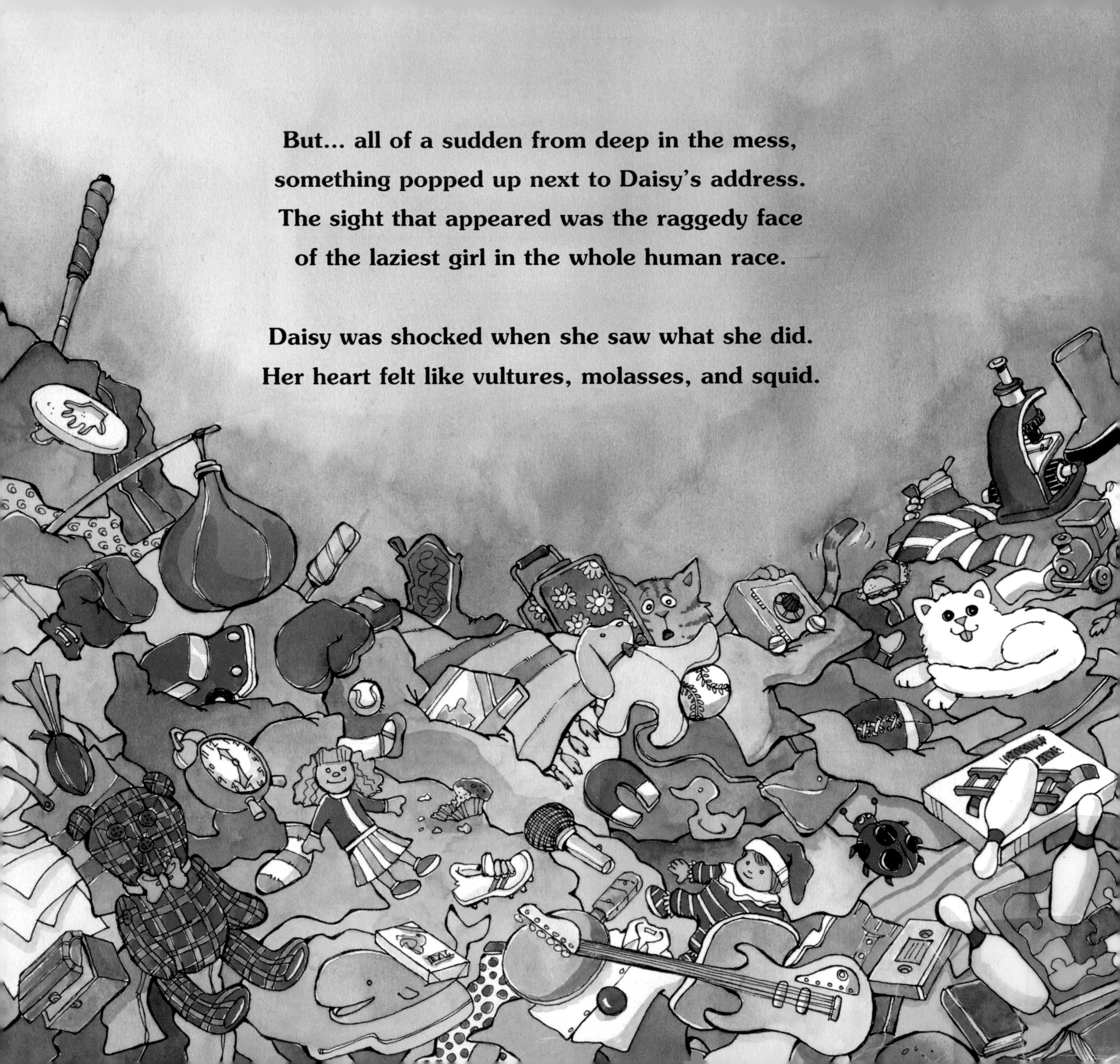

So she shrieked to the sky like a red squawking hen,
"I'LL NEVER, NOT EVER, BE LAZY AGAIN!!!"

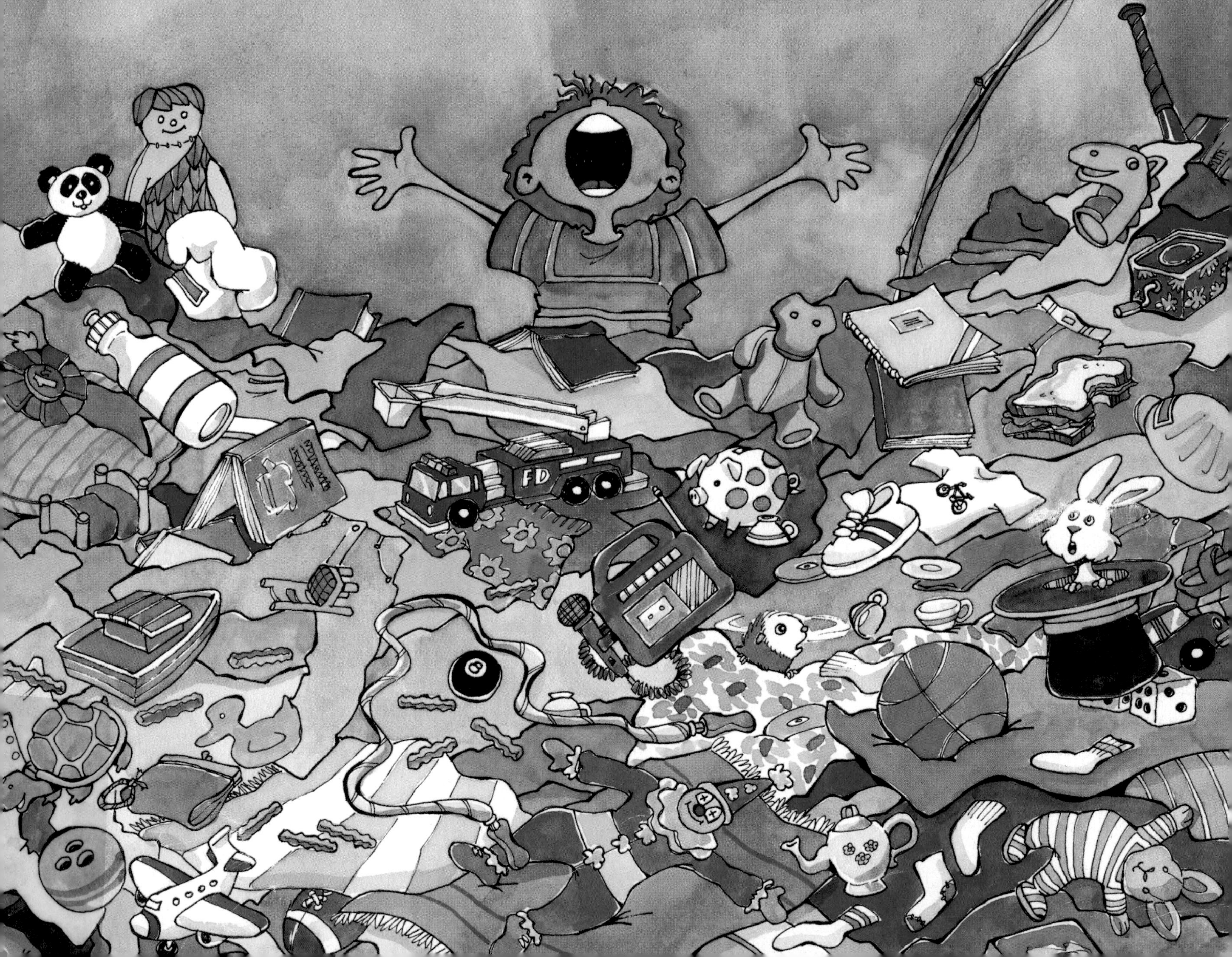
FD

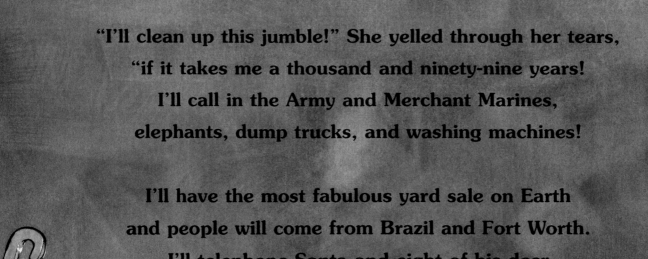

"I'll clean up this jumble!" She yelled through her tears,
"if it takes me a thousand and ninety-nine years!
I'll call in the Army and Merchant Marines,
elephants, dump trucks, and washing machines!

I'll have the most fabulous yard sale on Earth
and people will come from Brazil and Fort Worth.
I'll telephone Santa and eight of his deer
to haul off the clutter for Christmas next year!"

So Daisy began the incredible chore of cleaning her town 'til it shined like before.
The task wasn't easy, and some people say that Daisy's still working to this very day.

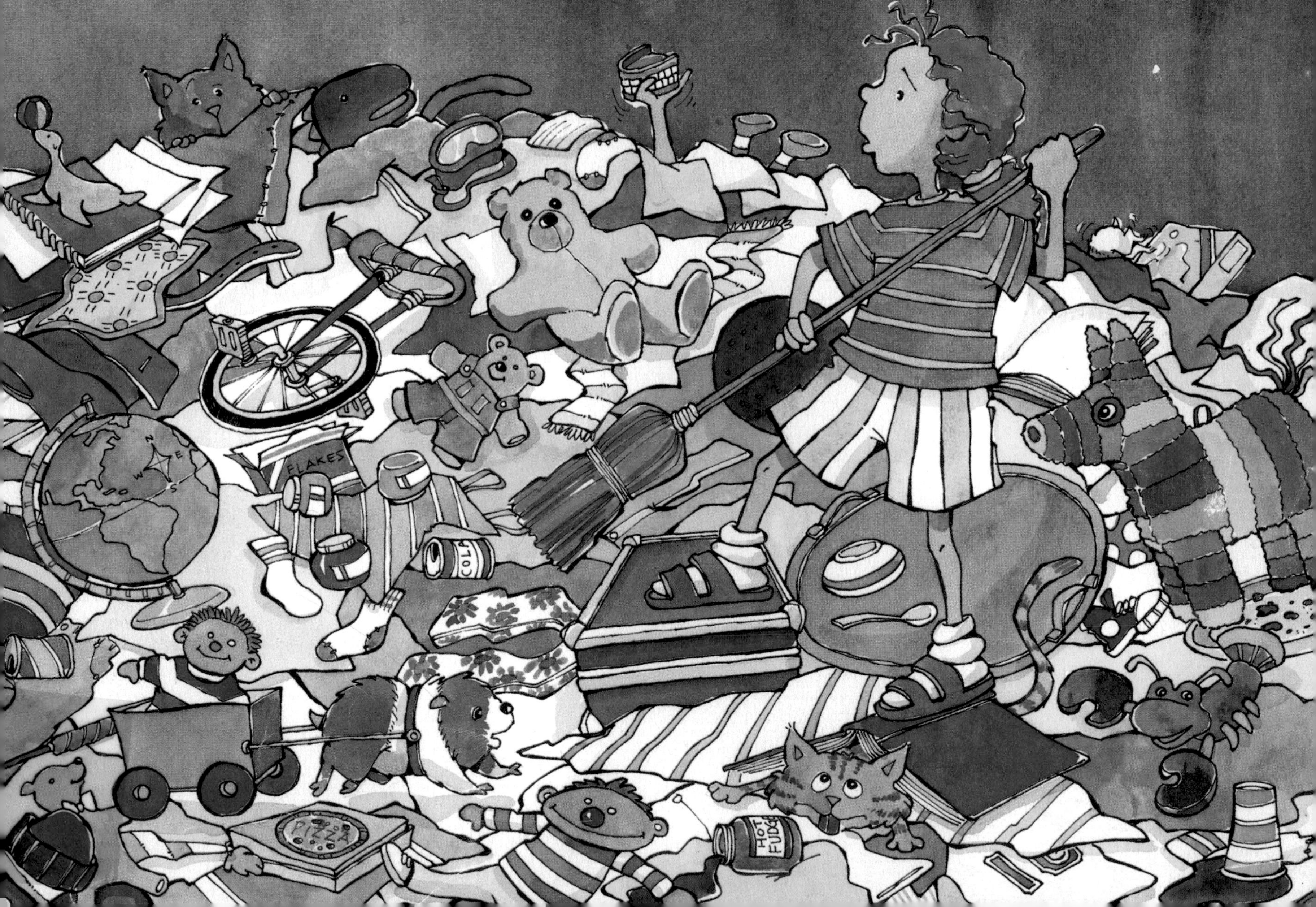
FLAKES
PIZZA
HOT FUDGE

So whether you're skinny or hairy or tall,

or live in Bermuda or southern St. Paul,

or Paris or Stinkwater Falls, Alabama,

for the sake of your city, your toys, and your Gramma,

in the name of bananas and earthworms and brooms,

get yourselves busy and clean up your rooms.